Suffer for This

Love, Sex, Marriage & Rock 'N' Roll

Suffer for This

Love, Sex, Marriage & Rock 'N' Roll

by Victor D. Infante

MOON
TIDE PRESS

~ 2024 ~

Editor-in-chief
Eric Morago

Editor Emeritus
Michael Miller

Marketing Specialist
Ellen Webre

Proofreaders
Jeremy Ra

Front & back cover art
Lea C. Deschenes

Author photo
Christine Peterson

Book design
Michael Wada

Moon Tide logo design
Abraham Gomez

Suffer for This: Love, Sex, Marriage & Rock 'N' Roll
is published by Moon Tide Press

Moon Tide Press
6709 Washington Ave. #9297
Whittier, CA 90608
www.moontidepress.com

FIRST EDITION

Printed in the United States of America

ISBN # 978-1-957799-22-3

To Lea, my best friend and editor, forever

Go to someone who lives in your heart. Now. Grab them by the shoulders or by the face or by the hand and look them in the eye. Say I love You. I. Love. You. Say I am thankful for You. Say You are a gift in my life. Say I accept all of You. I am ready to learn from You. I am ready to struggle for You. I am a child playing in the staggering presence of You. You. You. Say it. Now. Go.

— Sierra DeMulder

One

Because nothing happened. Because *nothing* happened. We find
suffering in the inflection of a word, the way we wrap our tongue
around a syllable. Love, we say, when we mean *love*. When we
mean a thousand pulses of blood, a thousand firing synapses.
When we mean the endorphin rush of a first kiss that leaves
us stoned and breathless, staggering alone from her doorway
to your car. Or when you see a woman across a crowded coffee
house, and know that you will have her – love as clairvoyance,
watching the origami of the future unfold, until you are drunk,
teeth clenched on her lip, until time falls forward again and you
are empty in a parking lot, reading the broken lines of your own
palm for some future that ends anywhere but there, and finding
none. Finding only inevitability, heartbreak and *want*.

We say love, but eschew definition, as though it were some
mason jar to store in a cupboard. Is love that blush of silence
that overwhelmed you in junior high school? The way her smile
still jars when you see it on some social-networking site online?
Is love the way a teenage girl's voice haunted you when you left
for college? the memory of a kiss in a park, children laughing in
the distance as they slid and swung, oblivious to the finality both
you and she saw reflected in each other's eyes, looming deadline
of distance, absence and blood which would, inevitably, boil
elsewhere? Is love the picture you keep in a box in the attic, the
one you haven't unearthed in years, but which you think about,
sometimes, on quiet nights when your wife sleeps soundly and
you have memorized the details of the ceiling?

I say all of this is love, and more. And less. I say love is the fact of
a person, the way she burns herself into the architecture of your
life. Love is what is both inevitable and durable. What burns and
heals and batters against your forehead and chest. Love is the
voice that will hush all others: each pretender, every demon.

And love is also none of this; but is instead the culmination of every love which has preceded it – mistake layered upon mistake, calculus of what the body needs and what the self no longer wishes to be. The attempt to rectify each faded mistake, to reclaim each ghost of what was right, without the reckoning and fall. This is love as we are *now*, this particular inflection of us.

Still, the voices still twitter in the distance. And still, there's a burning at the base of our skull.

Two

Mostly, my wife and I tell the story like this: We were at a music festival in a city where neither of us lived, in a crowd in front of an amphitheater. I told a joke. She was the only one who laughed. And that story's true, as far as it goes, but it's not precisely where it started. Not really. Merely prologue, a recognition of shared perspective. *A laugh in a crowd.* It wasn't a loud laugh, but it cut through the din, and when I turned to find its origin, I saw her on the steps above me — a tiny woman with Muppet-orange hair, glasses and a Tori Amos concert T-shirt — smiling, amused.

Sometimes, in private or with friends she doesn't mind scandalizing, the story extends further, with us in a hotel room, drinking Schlitz because it was all we could afford, talking music and poetry, politics and religion until familiar night falls on the unfamiliar city, and we're kissing on the edge of a rented bed and fucking in the bathroom, in case the friends she traveled with returned. What passes for discretion in youth. This serious business of marriage. *It started with a joke. She was the only one who laughed.*

I'd just finished dating a magician's assistant. She would vanish in a flurry of confusion and sleight-of-hand. My wife had been dating a ninja. He would cut and disappear. Both had a talent for shadows and silence. We were both off-balance. We both wanted nothing more than to vanish into music for a while. *It started with a joke.* It wasn't particularly funny.

Neither of us were skilled at disappearing. She had a boy orbiting her shyly. I met him briefly, in a bar, and liked him well-enough. Another woman and I were circling each other cautiously, kissing like thieves, navigating a thousand differences which blood was boiling to overcome. Blood is a stupid thing. It wants what it wants. Everything about her was straight-razor beautiful, even her smile, which could slice the skin off your cheek. One touch of her hand and I bled, but I was preoccupied with my empty wallet, my sputtering duct-taped car, my shabby bed in a rented room. She was nothing but kind, but I was frightened of the poverty in me, the way her beauty cast my failures into stark relief. And still, she consumed my thoughts for days, boiled my blood, until I made an awful joke, and only heard one laugh reply. And then (callously?) that boiling was gone.

It started with a joke. It started with the frantic, careless sex of young strangers in an unfamiliar city. It started with an amnesia of pulse, erasing everything that came before it, reducing each incarnation of love I'd known before to faded photographs, stored in a box in the attic of my heart. In the course of a day, she became an unshakable fact, and I was overwhelmed by the thought of losing her, of awakening to the negative space of her, to an absence which I knew, to my marrow, I'd eventually collapse into without her. Blood is a stupid thing, but it has its truths. She was a truth, and I crumbled before her and cried, confessed every failing and heartbreak, was the honest wretch of myself for perhaps the first time ever, and she touched my cheek and said nothing, and that is where our marriage began: in the absence of fear, in inexplicable trust, in a weeping honesty I'd never believed possible.

It started with a joke, it's true, but I've never known anything more serious.

Three

It started with a joke, and everything romantic comedies teach
say it should end here – mortgaged ranch house in the suburbs,
a reasonable commute. No children – not in the plan – but I think
I'm close to convincing my wife to adopt a shelter dog,
now that we have a yard. I only care that it's big and smart.
Neither of us like small, yappy dogs. She likes labs, but I want
a mutt. Mutts are smarter and healthier. Pure breads suffer
from genetic diseases, or so I'm told. Mutts have character, and
mutts at shelters frequently have histories. A smart mutt will
understand and value when it's safe and loved.

The house itself is nice, but unremarkable. The beige paint job is
recent, and serviceable. The front lawn is neat enough, although
I'll admit I'm careless about it. Never had a lawn before, and it
took a while to figure out the lawnmower. A neighbor showed me
how I had to push a button three times to prime the pump.
It was a mortifying way to introduce myself, but I grew up
in cites, where no one mows lawns and fewer people talk to
neighbors. I've never quite adjusted, never learned how to shed
that particular mask. Not wearing it is a sort of nudity. It feels
like everyone is staring.

I want to be a guy who likes mowing the lawn, a guy who's
handy and can use a hammer or band saw. I don't want to be
the guy who constantly asks for help. I've spent too much time
rebuilding myself. Doing it again sounds exhausting, but there
we are. Perhaps there are no endings, happy or otherwise.
Perhaps you just rebuild yourself and rebuild yourself until
something stops. And sometimes the changes come so fast that
the only one you think you can stomach is buying a dog.

The hypothetical dog is a constant source of breakfast conversation. Most weekend mornings, I wake up before my wife and put on a kettle, cook scrambled eggs, bacon and home fries. When the kettle goes off and I leave her tea to steep, she stumbles from the bedroom to the breakfast nook, wearing flannel pajamas and fuzzy slippers, Kodachrome hair tousled. If it's clean, I leave her the souvenir mug from the House on the Rock in Wisconsin, which we visited a few years back. I put on a second kettle to make myself coffee and claim the thick mug we got at a New Hampshire rest stop. If it's clean. We're terrible at dishes.

Sometimes, I suspect the only reason she won't commit to getting a dog is that she never had one as a kid. I had a whip-smart German shepherd who seemingly roamed our neighborhood freely, getting into mischief and stealing eclectic bits of food: Hot dog buns still in the wrapper, frozen hamburger patties, unopened bags of chips. It all sounds a little far-fetched, as though she were raiding picnics in the faraway suburbs, but it was the only dog I ever owned, so how am I to judge?

My wife tells me that she thinks leash laws have changed, and that you can't just let a dog roam anymore. I know, but somehow find it disappointing, although I'd be hard-pressed to tell you why.

In romantic comedies, the story ends with marriage, with the happy couple and their house and happy screaming children. We have a house and a hypothetical dog. And the torrid romance novels teach a different lesson, that when the story begins in domesticity, it ends in betrayal and despair.

And sometimes I wonder which type of story we're in, and try to decide if we're at the beginning or the end, until I realize that we're in the middle, and the kettle's boiling for the second time, and the eggs are burning, and there's a dog howling in the distance.

Four

I've unearthed two personal truths in the archaeology of how and why I love: The first is that the girl next door is, for me, an unhealthy archetype, and the second is that there is a lake of silence burbling beneath my every word and action. Not a *placid* lake – the surface ripples unprovoked, as though something were stirring in its depths, something primordial. This is the heart as Loch Ness Monster, impossible creature we joke about, but whose existence we find ourselves believing wholeheartedly in the dark of the night: Impossible thing we know exists. This is the heart as an atheists' God: Faint whisper in the wind, flash of insight into underlying structure, denied by morning's light.

First date ever, 16 years old: She was nice in the way that begs disbelief, the way you can't help but guess is a construction, masking … something. You have no idea what, except that you know your own masks, know they muffle a scream that extends back to the cradle, a scream that's been there so long you find it comforting. It's why you choke on words sometimes, bury yourself in silence. You know what's stirring in the lake of yourself, what you don't want rising to the surface. You convince yourself it's the same for everybody, and the thought that it might *not* be becomes the first of a thousand differences you perceive between yourself and everybody else. That suspicion becomes the first of many silences.

We stared at each other across the plastic table of a food court Chinese take-out. We broke a Guinness world record for sitting awkwardly. We turned 45 minutes into a sound-free island where time stood still. Civilizations rose and toppled in our silence, whole species fell into extinction. Our silence was comets pelting the Earth over and over and over again, until all that was left of mankind were the patrons of a bar in Northern Uzbekistan, who missed the whole thing because they'd had the good sense to get drunk beforehand.

Dan Rather commented on the silence on live television, calling it, "The worst date in the history of dating." I could hear Dan speaking to a frightened nation, saying "I have seen the grim realities of war, America. In Vietnam, I saw things that brought grown men weeping to their knees. But America, believe me when I tell you that I have never, *ever* seen anything as painful as *this*."

We nibbled at egg rolls. We fiddled with chopsticks. I looked long into the lo mein. The lo mein looked long into me. Finally, we talked about homework. We had both read the T.S. Eliot. We talked about *The Wasteland*, and *Prufrock*. We were enacting an interpretive dance of *The Wasteland* and *Prufrock*. She was kind when she said goodbye. There was no kiss, no hug, just a smile that shined with sincerity, and something I now recognize as pity, leaving me alone with the oracle of half-eaten noodles, which held no answers.

There were no John Hughes movie cliches. She did not avoid me in the halls. She spoke to me easily, mostly about school. She was *nice*, and I no longer distrusted that niceness. I was embarrassed, yes, but I also felt a sort of gratitude. Still do. There was no second chance at love, nor did we become best friends. We co-existed easily, floating in a void devoid of any real possibility or motion.

Nearly two years later, after I had just been dumped by my first real girlfriend, I asked her to prom on a whim. She informed me she was already going with a meathead jock who had once punched me by the lockers for no reason when I was younger and weaker. My phrasing, obviously, not hers. I furrowed my brow when she told me but constructed a mask to hide the silence snowing in my head, to guard a disapproval I had no right in owning. I smiled and shrugged, and she smiled with a kindness now devoid of pity. I ended up not going.

When I saw her the Monday after the dance, she didn't seem to have enjoyed herself. There was something different about her smile, something guarded, conspicuous only because I had never seen her wear a mask before.

Five

There is a sense that every wedding exists in the eye of a hurricane, tiny island amid wind and devastation. We say *it started with a joke*, or that *it started with a kiss*, but a marriage is a series of beginnings, and so it also started *here*, with a hundred people we love huddled in ocean-side cottages, waiting for a break in the wind and rain, expensive shoes kicked to the side as a nervous bride calculates the damage of damp sand to the train of her dress, weighs whether she wishes to marry with mud-caked feet.

It's no different for anyone. A wedding is a convergence of winds. We flurry invitations and seating charts, registries and reservations; invite the cynical clucks and drunken misadventures of awkward relatives into the cathedral of our hearts and pray that the destruction they have always sewn will subside a moment. Or we run away to Vegas or Atlantic City, stirring a different sort of chaos entirely, but still, we love on the edge of a storm, and still we navigate our way toward its eye. And we think of the cake, or the deejay, or anything but an endless tomorrow that stretches out against a storm-tossed sky.

I feel small beneath the thrift-store umbrella, soggy as I move from cottage to cottage. Our parents talk uncomfortably of nothing, her father's eyes fixed at the looming clouds. Elsewhere, an uncle has uncovered the scotch reserved for later. Well-meaning friends comment on the height of the surf, joke that they wish they had brought their boards. Someone has already snuck off for a joint. I find Schrödinger's bride, like her father, watching the skies, repeating radio reports that the storm will be blowing out to sea. I smile, but say nothing, and instead pull her close, gentle as to not wrinkle the dress.

She seems unaware that she is already a subsided storm, the break of sunlight across black clouds, the revelation of a sky which was always present but seemed forever out of reach. *How can she not know that?* I think, and she smiles, pecks my lips and touches her palm to my cheek, as if to answer my unasked question.

I pull away and spy my wife's artist friend watching us too closely, mist swelling in her eyes, her gaze following the contours of the expectant bride's neck and shoulders. I put the thought aside, still dimly cautious of looming storms. Everywhere around us is the ruckus of family and friends, the collision of two lives that were in no way waiting patiently for one another. We both have our histories and would have continued as such had we never met. It's not a comforting thought, this cold dismissal of fairy tales and destiny. Somewhere, a voice chides that this wedding could have happened just as easily in a church, and I think to myself that that would have in no way stopped the rain, but replying is pointless. A friend jokes that there's always the justice of the peace, another cracks that it's not too late to run. I laugh politely but can't help but think that this wedding is simply an acknowledgment of something that's been true for years, a synchronized orbit, a fact.

The sky turns calm, and we parade to the beach. There are storm clouds in the distance, but otherwise the sky is as blue as I ever seen it. I stand with the lolling ocean touching the edge of my shoes. The cellist we'd hired plays *Here Comes the Bride*, and I turn to face her, the sunlight glinting off her hair. All the din of family and friends, the hundred people we love whom also, sometimes, drive us crazy, subsides like rain clouds, and even the wind stills. I taste brine each time I say the words I'm asked to repeat. *Do You*, and *in sickness and in health*, and *I do*. They're not just words, and this is not just salt on my lips. And when I kiss her, even the ocean fades away.

Six

A wedding is not a marriage. It's the start of a marriage, and as I've said, it's only *one* beginning. My wife and I were married long before our wedding. We lived for years in the same space, developing an instinctive orbit. There was gravity there before the acknowledgment of legal paperwork and ceremony. Some people go forever like that, whether by choice or cruel legal quirk, married in every way that matters. And others are married in name only, their lives lived separately under one roof. It's easy to sign papers and pay fees, easy to say *I do*, but that is not a marriage. It is not so easy to surrender the concept of *I* for the concept of *we*. It is hard to stop seeing yourself as your *self*, first. When love is a slow, cool river, that melding comes naturally, almost unnoticed. *I do not know much about gods*, wrote Eliot, *but I think that the river Is a strong brown god.*

I don't know much about God, in the Christian sense, but I have a sense of provenance, of – having bathed in it – recognizing when that river runs true and deep. Marriage is the thing that is left in the kiln when new passion's heat is cooled, when two people give themselves over to the river. Call that river God, if you will. I won't disagree, for what is God but the totality of everything, that moment in union when everything is possible, because everything is one breath. Or call it nothing at all, mere arithmetic. Whatever it is, it is the fact of two people, and of love, and of a transubstantiation of what two people were into something else entirely.

And yet, a marriage doesn't change you at all. When the ceremony's finished and the newly married couple's kiss becomes a series of photos in albums, when the guests have finished their drinks, eaten cake, danced to some atrocious song and evaporated back into their normal lives, the married couple are still themselves, their wants and histories, passions and pasts still burbling beneath the surface. The wedding itself is not a magic trick. It changes nothing. It is only the wanting to change that makes it so.

Seven

The first time my wife and I saw the house, sunlight streamed through bay windows into the empty living room, making the freshly waxed hard-wood floors glisten. The entire place seemed impossibly large. I couldn't imagine our lives expanding enough to fill it. Part of me even questioned trying.

There is a finality in emptiness, the perfection of its desolation. Or maybe that emptiness is a beginning. They look remarkably similar, depending on your perspective. In any case, marring the emptiness seemed ... significant. Whatever happened next, that particular *tabula rasa* would now be forever out of reach.

We filled the space with cardboard boxes begged from a grocery store we will no longer shop at when we move. It felt like asking for a parting gift. Then more boxes from the Barnes & Noble down our old street, which remains the bookstore physically closest to us, then some from the Best Buy we rarely ever visit – just when we needed new computer accouterments. We finally bought more boxes from U-Haul. They were more expensive than we'd like, but scrounging was starting to wear us out.

Every artifact of our lives is boxed and crammed into a rented truck. The futon bed we swore we'd replace a year or two before, the beaten-down blue couch we bought from a friend for fifty bucks, the oddly sturdy green entertainment center my wife's aunt found at a yard sale: All our shabby furnishings lumber with us, their cheapness even more evident against the blank canvas house. Every other possession we own is stuffed into boxes, stacked haphazardly in the living room before being sorted, dispersed to the corners of the house. Part of me disbelieves we'll ever be able to fill it. This emptiness and permanence terrifies me. I watch the sun dance on the edges of blinds my wife says we'll replace as soon as possible, and disbelieve I will ever have enough inside of me to fill a home.

Eight

I was sometimes the villain of the piece. That was never my intention, but I suppose it rarely is.

Nine

17, the letter X streaked in black marker on the back of each of
my hands. The music is loud and distorted. My head is static.
I stop listening for nuance and just allow my bones to rattle.
I ignore my ears entirely, and learn to listen with my blood,
staring transfixed from the back of the nightclub, gaze drawn
to an alien world. Near the stage, large boys slam hard against
each other, laugh raucously and bounce maniacally. Rhythm is a
coincidence. Synchronization comes with abandon, surrendering
to the violent torrent. The chord structures are simple. This isn't
lost on me. The whirlwind surrounding me? That's simple, too.
Everything surrounding me is primal. Everything surrounding
me is *change*. The only thing preventing me from surrendering to
the maelstrom is a well of fear in my stomach, a looming dread
of embarrassment, like I could do something wrong in a room
where everyone is crashing madly like some lunatic tide against
a craggy shoreline. Best to do nothing. Best to disappear into the
background. Become wallpaper.

I almost didn't get in the car when my friend asked me to go.
There was homework to do, and television. There was the
security of a bed and a tiny room where I could predict the
nothing that would happen. There was a fear that enveloped
me like a blanket, paralysis born of … *something*. Some film
of emotion that coated my throat, some staccato tune playing
loudly and out of time on the flipside of my chest. My friend was
coming here to see a girl, and didn't want to come alone. He was
no less awkward than I was, no less the bruised shell of locker
room beatings and late nights reading comic books, vocabulary of
Dungeons & Dragons and Rush songs sung loudly in his mother's
garage. It wasn't a *date*. She hung out there often, dancing to
bands who knew no discernible beat. It was an act of bravery for
him to come. I couldn't deny him that.

We never saw her. He disappeared into the pit, diving in like it were the ocean, like this flail of dancing were perfectly natural. And maybe it was. Maybe it's the stubborn reticence that's abnormal, the act of willing one's self invisible when it's not at all necessary, behaving like prey in a place where there's no real predator. I didn't know that yet. Didn't know that — in the real world — most people are usually content to ignore you. I hadn't figured out yet that this cacophony of noise and sweat *was* the real world, that the schoolyards where they lock you away with the bullies and the sociopaths was actually the abomination.

There was a girl leaning against the wall near me, staring transfixed at the band as they writhed and screamed and hit things to produce bewildering noise. She wore black lipstick and a crushed velvet dress. He hair was dyed onyx, and in the dim lights of the club she was almost invisible — flash of pale skin as she leaned from shadow to shadow. My blue jeans and T-shirt itched, my skin suddenly aware that the acceptably trendy brand name was no longer camouflage.

She said something, and I couldn't make it out above the din. She moved closer, to no avail. Finally, she pressed her lips against mine. They tasted of alcohol and lemon. Blood rushed my head, and for a moment, my mind was clear. The cacophony receded, and the only thing that was real was this sleight girl whose name I didn't know, this girl whose words kept disappearing into tuneless guitars. I pulled her close and kissed her again. And there was no music, no din of bodies, no *time*. The moment hung there, our tongues hungrily seeking each other, the only audible sound a heartbeat that could have been hers, or mine, or both. And then the song ended, and she threw her head back and laughed. Not a mocking laugh, just a release of joy. She leaned forward again, pecked me once more on the lips, then disappeared into the crowd. I moved to follow, but she was gone.

Stunned, I searched the club for her, but she was nowhere to be found. I never saw her again. This was before I knew there were women who would kiss just to kiss, to capture some electricity of feeling. That it was not a promise or an invitation or anything more than the moment it was. This was before I knew anything at all, save a loneliness which had, for one brief moment, abated entirely — drowned in the sea of endorphins swimming my head, skin tingling. The world seemed far away, the raucous music the only thing that broke through. And it didn't seem like noise anymore. It made a strange, inexplicable sense.

I never saw that girl again. Eventually, my friend emerged from the crowd, never having found the girl he was chasing, but brimming with newfound joy. He talked excitedly, but I just nodded, not really listening. We left the club, exiting onto the neon-lit street outside, and I was silent for a good long while, part of me searching the crowded nicotine haze outside for the first girl I'd ever kissed, part of me already forgetting her, surrendering her to the chaos of the night. Finally, as we walked to the car, a sentence formed on my tongue, before I had even consciously pondered the words.

"I think I want to play the guitar," I said, although it was nothing I had ever thought or wanted before. And as I said the words, the memory of that kiss resurfaced, and I knew they would always be entwined.

We'd return to that club often, but she was a ghost. No one I ever met knew her. Even now, I sometimes look at photos from those times that friends have posted on the Web, searching the backgrounds for a glimpse of her face, some tangible proof that this person was real. But to no avail. It was just a moment — life-changing, in its way, at least for me — but gone like smoke.

My friend and the girl he was chasing eventually got together, and I saw them both less frequently for a while. One night, she gave me a ride home from the club, and we sat in her car on the street in front of my house, and she broke down crying. She told me he'd be stoned most nights now, how she was only there at all because he was off shooting up with some friends somewhere else, on the other side of the din and noise. She told me she wasn't sure how he was paying for the junk, but there was something in the way she phrased it that made me think she knew more than she admitted, and that saying it was overwhelming. I was silent, knowing nothing of this, unsure of how I'd missed it entirely.

Then she kissed me, and a voice in the back of my head screamed for me to stop, but I ignored it as we clutched at each other — kissing sloppily, desperately in the front seat of a worn-down sedan, my hand groping her breast, hers rubbing my thigh. We sat there, pawing one another for an hour, before finally she said she had to go, and I went inside to my too-small room and stared at the ceiling until daylight cracked through the window.

My friendship with both of them receded then, tide ebbing away from shore. I bought a guitar, began to teach myself how to play.

Ten

If you were to ask, and I were to answer honestly — both unlikely prospects — I would tell you that I am a dog who has been heeling for almost 20 years, that fidelity has a mass that rests on your chest. And yet, I make no movement to assuage that weight, its burden seeming a small price to pay. When I am honest — and really, I only find that honesty in solitude — I can admit that weight is far less cumbersome than the loneliness I used to carry. I don't know if it's because fidelity is lighter, or if it's because I'm no longer carrying the loneliness. I can't tell from this perspective. It's a jagged piece of sky from a narrow window slit. I only see the flash of blue, the occasional cloud. The entirety of the vista is beyond me, from where I'm standing.

I *do* know the loneliness is only abated, not vanished completely. It hits me at odd-angles, small car crashes on desolate streets, not reported in the morning's paper, put out of mind entirely, save for the strange fear of discovery, a shuddering shame germinating from unsolicited want, unacknowledged, not acted upon, but visceral nonetheless. Substantive enough to bruise my ribs, dull pain aching for release.

When I was younger, the loneliness was palpable enough to hold full sway, to abandon judgment, succumb to a want that seemed to have its own mind. *Blood is a stupid thing. It wants what it wants.* And so I kissed a friend's ex-girlfriend in a gas station parking lot, the impulse sparking so hot I feared for the gas tanks. And so my fingers entwined with another friend's fiance, allowed my hands to return her caresses in silence, as we fell into one another in a wordless evening of which we'd never speak again. And so I stole embraces with another woman, behind a coffeehouse I frequented, until a conversation with her young daughter convinced me that I wasn't ready to be the man she needed me to me. I replaced love with prestidigitation: Presto! Nothing up my sleeve! It was only a cunning illusion, only ever sleight of hand.

The dalliances came and went, as they do with the young, and all the while it never occurred to me that I might be doing *harm* — to them, to the people around us, to *myself.* I was an actor pantomiming my way through a script written by my own restless skin. Or perhaps *their* skin, as I do not recall with any clarity whose lips first touched whose, whose hand first reached across a darkened room, the order of kisses that appeared unannounced, relieving the weight I suffered under, if only for a moment. I had my history, and they did too, and it's odd how, despite the moments' intensity, that we remain mere bit parts in each other's movies. And it's odd how I never really *forget* any of them, how they mean something, even now.

The memory of each firefly romance is part of the mosaic, the framework of how and why I love. And perhaps the reverse is true. I've long since lost touch with most of them, even forgotten several of their names. I do no know what place the mistake of me holds in their hearts. Perhaps it's best if I never do.

And still the loneliness appears from time to time, and I wonder if it's really loneliness at all, or something else I have no name for. I hear their voices in the back of my head, recounting lessons I've already learned.

Eleven

The heart learns the darkest lessons first: The way its pounding drowns out circumspection, the way blood quickens before one learns control. To be young is to be part monster: The first stirrings belong to the villain. There is simply *want* and nothing else.

My wife has a prom picture in the photo album. She's 15 or 16, in a tight, powder blue dress that clings to her body. She wears it cavalierly, as only teenagers can. Her hair is its natural blonde, permed in the unfortunate '80s style. She is beautiful: The photo captures her flickering between girlishness and adulthood. Her smile is bright and genuine.

Her date is awkward angles and floppy arms. Seeing them together, I can only imagine his purpose was to ward off crows. I do not share this observation with my wife, but the first time I saw the photo she had to strain to remember anything about the boy. Even his name seemed a distant echo. She looks like she's enjoying herself in the picture. He looks a little lost. In that, the scarecrow has my sympathy. He is easily two or three years older than her, but there is no real burgeoning manhood in his body, all height and elbows. He is a boy, as I was a boy at his age.

And in all honesty, one imagines my wife was just a girl, although the villain in me stirs at the photograph, covets the unfamiliar terrain of the body I know best. I choke the thought down, lock it away deep in my body, bury it in darkness and bile. It sits in my stomach until I am seasick. The villain has scratched too closely at the skin.

My heart learned loneliness first, and thirst, and when it found lips to kiss and breasts to grope and the static shock of flesh against flesh, it didn't want to lose them. Fear suits the villain, convinces you this is the last time you'll ever be touched. That you will lose this feeling forever. Everything is new, and impermanent.

It's terribly odd to feel guilty for lusting for the echo of my wife ambered in a fading photograph. More than 20 years later, feeling guilty for pawing my friend's girlfriend doesn't feel abnormal at all. *That* guilt is burned into my memory, my original sin, although hardly my last.

My childhood best friend was a junkie, and I somehow had missed this transformation. I don't know how that happened. We both leaped into the same unknowable abyss, and landed in completely different places. I was so deeply immersed in Ramones and Minor Threat albums that I never noticed he had disappeared. I heard somewhere he had found God after graduation, that he was living in the Midwest someplace. I never saw either him or his girlfriend again after high school. I'm not even friends with either on Facebook. I'm well aware that *I'm* the one who turned away.

My wife doesn't know what became of the scarecrow, just that he never made a deep impression. She's disinterested in the question, in the photograph with the first flaring of music video hair. If she spends any time pondering might-have-beens, she's never vocalized it. She's far too practical for that, this blunt, unshockable woman who values honesty above all else, who wickedly delights sometimes when the truth makes people squirm.

She is right in front of me. She is *always* in my line of vision. And still, I look at the photograph and pant for her youth, when I know full-well that what's really shaking me is the realization that, no matter how forthright she always is, there are pieces of her that I will never know.

Twelve

My first real girlfriend was an MTV VJ: Vibrant, unfailingly cheerful and cooler than I'd ever be. From this vantage, she's an impossibly distant memory. Sometimes, I barely believe she existed. I met her at guitar lessons. We had the same teacher and would exchange smiles and hellos as I left my session and she began hers. I had a starter acoustic guitar, bought cheap at Sears — I don't even recall the brand. It had an adequate sound, I suppose, except when *I* played it. When *I* played it, it creaked and hissed like a water-logged cat. Our teacher had a penchant for Beatles songs, and I fumbled my way through *We Can Work It Out* and *Day Tripper*, hitting most of the notes in the right order, but with no sense of timing whatsoever. I was — and I knew this — truly awful, and yet I persevered, because playing guitar was the most free I had ever felt. Butchering the Lennon-McCartney songbook was the only time I felt alive. I wanted to play amplified power chords in four-four time. My teacher would have settled for my playing *anything* in four-four time.

She was tiny and bright — peculiarly happy, to the point of credulity. She wore her blonde hair in a ponytail, tied back with a bright, pink scrunchie. It was always the scrunchie that people remembered her by, although that strikes me as one of her less striking bits of style. She wore jeans and T-shirts with the logos of then-popular bands — The Cure, The Smiths, Depeche Mode. I knew she was a year behind me at school but didn't know her particularly well. She had a toothpaste commercial smile: I could lose myself in it, and in her gleaming blue eyes.

Talking to girls was still near-impossible. I'd go see bands, or occasionally even go to parties, and still my voice vanished when I felt an iota of *want*. If I wanted *nothing*, it was fine. But if my heart skipped a beat, if I saw a moment of possibility, the silence clenched my throat and my voice vanished, like magic. *Nothing up my sleeve*, says the moose. *Again?* says the Squirrel. *But that trick never works.*

It occurred to me, eventually, that she had surely been listening outside the door each time I mangled *Get Back* or *Got To Get You Into My Life*. At first, this was a little horrifying. I imagined her near-omnipresent smile stretching into a grimace as I plucked at the strings. Then, slowly, it motivated me to improve, until one night I managed a serviceable rendition of *We Can Work It Out*. My teacher, for the first time, looked more pleased than patient.

We smiled at each other as always as we crossed paths, and if there was any difference in her smile after my middling success, I couldn't perceive it. Still, I lingered afterward, to listen to her play from behind the safety of a closed door. She worked her way through a flawless *Yesterday* — including vocals — that had the teacher clapping afterward. It made sense, actually. Even though she was younger than me, she'd probably started playing well before. I left quietly, my earlier musical triumph eclipsed by the realization that she was out of my league. Which was to say, she was *in* a league. I resolved to become a better player. She continued to smile when we passed. It would be weeks of blistering my fingers before I found out that smile meant anything.

Thirteen

It's not as if I was unaware of rock 'n' roll as a teenager. That would have been impossible in the '80s, unless you were Amish or lived in one of a handful of scattered rural enclaves where the radio only caught Gospel stations and the occasional Hank Williams tune. My earliest childhood memories include spastic dancing, flailing joyously to my mother's Four Tops and Supremes albums. Even then, I could feel something palpable in the music, something solid and alive that I could almost touch. Motown made me deliriously happy, but it was always someone else's music. It was always borrowed from my mother.

And still, latchkey-locked while she was at work, I'd dig through the musical record of her teenage years, thrilling to Bob Dylan, Aretha Franklin and Janis Joplin. And to the Beatles. More than anything, the Beatles. My mother had everything, even their solo albums. I was drawn to album covers: The menacing silver space alien adorning the 8-track of Ringo Starr's *Goodnight, Vienna* grabbed my attention, although the music never stayed with me. Not the way *Octopus' Garden* or *I Get By With A Little Help From My Friends* stayed with me. I was amused by the silliness of Paul McCartney's *Band on the Run*, the way the songs just changed for seemingly no reason. I remember when my mother bought the then-newly released John Lennon album, *Double Fantasy*. I couldn't deal with the Yoko One songs, and didn't understand why he would put them on the album in the first place. Even my mother skipped them.

There were a couple Rolling Stones albums in her collection, and at least one by the Doors, but the newer music, the music of her young adulthood – Roberta Flack, James Taylor, Carly Simon, Elton John – didn't interest me at all. As an adult, I'd find virtues in some of these artists, but that would be years in the future. As a kid, all I knew was *like* and *dislike*, and I disliked them with an unfettered, unfiltered certainty, complaining mightily if my mother played them on the stereo, until she either relented or banished me to my room. The soft rock and "adult contemporary" of the early '70s became closely associated with punishment.

I craved background noise as a child, a constant buzz to ward off loneliness. If there was nothing interesting on television, I'd turn on the radio as I read comic books. It kept me company while I sank into Spider-Man or Batman's adventures. The routine was comforting: Come home from school, throw down my book bag, grab a soda from the refrigerator, turn on the radio and plop on the couch. It didn't even much matter what was on the radio, until one day – as I was settling in to read my first of what would be a seeming lifetime of the Avengers' pulse-pounding confrontations with the android super villain Ultron – I was faced with something too horrible to bear:

Why do birds/ suddenly appear/ every time you are near ….

Oh, Karen Carpenter. I knew nothing of your tragic life, and had no regard for your beautiful voice. All my pre-teen brain knew was that I hated you more than any super villain has ever hated any superhero. More than the Joker hated Batman, more than the Green Goblin hated Spider-Man, more than Ultron hated *everybody*. I hated this song more than I had ever hated any one of the numerous school bullies I'd endured. The song was like a cheese grater scraping across my ears. My entire body recoiled at the sound.

... just like me/ they long to be/ close to you ....

It was too awful to endure, and far too distracting to tune out while I read, so I did the unthinkable, and changed the station on my mother's radio. A few clicks and some static, and I realized I hadn't checked to see what station it was originally on, and I wondered idly if my mother would be mad. Would *she* ever be able to find that station again? But I suspected she knew the number. I didn't. I just dialed past commercials and sports until I found some music I didn't hate. Which was when I discovered something new:

We don't need no education/ we don't need no thought control ...

The song was like nothing I'd ever heard before, and nothing like anything my mother owned.

... no dark sarcasm in the classroom ...

The radio seemed too small for the sound emerging. I listened wordlessly, not fidgeting, leaving the Avengers neglected on the coffee table.

Hey! Teacher! Leave those kids alone!

I didn't know what the song was, nor had I ever heard of Pink Floyd, but somehow, in the eccentric clockwork of my 9-year-old brain, I knew I had discovered something: A music that was indelibly *mine*. Plans unfolded in my head: I would ask my mother for a cassette player for Christmas, so I could listen to music in my room. I'd save up my allowance for tapes.

I had no idea that within a month, John Lennon would be dead, and my mother—heartbroken and listening to *Double Fantasy* straight through – would stop seeking out new music altogether. I had no idea that the '70s where now truly, irrevocably over. I had no idea that something new had already begun.

Fourteen

When we moved into our house, my wife developed a passion
for gardening — one I never quite shared. After years of city
apartments, she relished the chance to get her hands dirty, to
coax things into growing. Sometimes, I think to tell her she
helped *me* to grow, but it sounds too sappy, even for me. I've
become somewhat soppy as I've aged, trying to fill that space
where fear and anxiety used to live with love, to hold onto it at
all costs. I never let a day go by without telling her I love her, but
sometimes, I wonder if she can sense the demons that I've pushed
to the recesses of my brain. I imagine she can.

She has her *own* demons, of course. She had a life before we met.
And yet, it's hard for me to envision her past lovers — even
those I've met — as anything more than shadow puppets on
the wall. I imagine the reverse is true, too. We had no friends
in common when we met, no shared history. I know some of
her stories, but that's not the same as having watched her date
another man from afar, if we had traveled in the same circles like
some sit-com couple, a will-they, won't-they Ross and Rachel.
We were thunderclap sudden. We were lightning arcing across
an empty sky. Sometimes, it's hard to remember life before her.
I inadvertently edit her into scenes where she wasn't present.
That time I saw *Jesus Christ Superstar*, for example? That was
with a lovely blonde art student I dated for a while after college,
but sometimes I ask my wife if she remembers something from
the play — the flamboyant Herod, for example, with his Carmen
Miranda headdress — forgetting that she wasn't there. Memory
is a less reliable tool than one would hope. All narrators are,
to some degree, unreliable.

I could not tell you of her first kiss or her first fuck. I'm sure she's spoken of them — she's never been the retiring type — but the details never settle in my brain. They were with boys whose names I don't know, whose faces I would never recognize. She tells a story of her father finding her with a boy in her room, and his quite literally throwing him out of the house. I know about the boy in college who O.D.'d, and the two women she fucked in her early 20s. I know she was engaged for a while to a man who tried to wall her off from the world, so constricted she could barely breathe. I'm sure, if I thought about it, I could dredge the details of these stories and others from the recesses of my brain, but at some point, I would be conflating events, filling in bits to make the story flow. And they're not *my* stories. I have no business telling them, save to say that they are what's made her the person she is, even as my own shaped *me*. Still, those stories are half the equation of how we learned to love the way we do, and I will only ever understand them academically. They remain a movie which I was told about, but never saw. I only know the person she was when I met her, and the person she is *now*.

She was a painter when we met, and now she's a graphic designer. I was a guitarist when we met, and now I work for a PR firm and write freelance record reviews in my spare time. She rarely paints anymore, although occasionally the mood strikes her and she sets up a canvas on the back porch. We have a few on our walls. She gives them to friends, sometimes, or locks them in the attic. Likewise, I rarely pick up the guitar and play anymore, even in private, and my days of playing in front of audiences are done. Those days seem far away, though I can sometimes remember them in my skin, fingers fretting the air, silently playing some old Clash or Elvis Costello song.

Sometimes, I'll sit on the back porch, have a cigarette, and watch my wife in the garden, pulling weeds and planting seeds. Once in a while, I'll come help, although I'm really only good for brute force. I tamed the Japanese knot weed on the side of the house by ripping each plant from the ground. It was strangely satisfying. Mostly, though, I just watch her, watch the focus and purpose gardening brings. It's captivating. I marvel at her. I always have.

Fifteen

I had no money as a teenager. My mother worked long hours at
a call center, before those all moved to other countries. My father
died when I was young. I didn't drive and walked everywhere.
Walking miles was no big deal to me, actually, except when I had
to carry my guitar. At those times, I needed rides, or took the
bus. Taking the bus with a guitar is as ridiculous at it sounds.
It takes its own seat. It draws attention to you, which I suppose
is its job, but some places one actually *prefers* to remain invisible.
You're *never* invisible with a guitar in your hand.

To pay for guitar lessons, I worked part-time at a convenience
store, one of the ones that made you wear a tacky orange and
green jacket. It was, on the whole, innocuous, although I tired of
kids who never spoke to me in school hitting me up to let them
buy beer. Their attention wasn't worth it to me. It would have
endangered my guitar lessons. And it would have endangered my
small moments of exchanging smiles with the MTV VJ who'd
soon be my first girlfriend. Not that I knew that, then. Despite
surviving the WORST DATE EVER, and despite a random kiss
in a club, I still felt uneasy asking anyone out. I couldn't afford to
take a girl to dinner, or to a movie, or just about anything. That
sort of poverty has a weight. It colors everything you do.

So I was surprised when she caught me leaving school one day and asked *me* if I wanted to go downtown and get a root beer float. Seriously … *a root beer float.* Everything took on a psychedelic quality. Time distorted, and everything seemed muffled and distant, as though I were watching myself from far away. I don't recall ever saying *yes*, but instead just sort of casually accompanied her downtown, where we ordered floats in a '50s-style diner, Buddy Holly's voice echoing across decades. The Norman Rockwell of it all only made it more surreal. She talked the whole time, mostly about guitars and music. I told her about the punk club I had started going to, about how it inspired me to pick up the guitar. She told me I was pretty good for a beginner. I laughed out loud. She was *amazing*, and I told her so. She had been playing since she was little, when she found her father's guitar and started strumming on it, pretending to be a rock star.

I walked her to her house, and she kissed me — just a peck on the cheek — before disappearing inside. I sleepwalked home, head buzzing, barely able to register what had just happened.

Over the next few weeks, we talked a lot, and sometimes even managed to go to the beach or catch a movie. It didn't seem to matter that I didn't have any money, although I quietly began to fret as prom approached — I had never thought much about it before, and now it seemed something I was obligated to consider. Mostly, though, we played music, me struggling to keep up with her, weaving our way through classic rock favorites. We would play a Bob Dylan song, or something by the Stones, and then we'd make out, pawing each other tentatively. And all the while I wondered where the boundary was, how far my hand was allowed to careen down her back, how close to her breasts I was allowed to come. Each encounter found my hands edging closer and closer to those unacknowledged boundaries. But there was always a line, a sense that I shouldn't push things too far, too fast. Which, in retrospect, is a fairly amazing insight for a teenager.

I saved for prom, unsure if I'd be able to make it. I didn't much care about it, but I wanted her to have a good time. I wanted this to go on forever.

One evening, after school, we noodled our way through some Cure songs, which sounded odd on acoustic guitars, but not distractingly so. We finished *Let's Go To Bed* and fell over laughing. My hand reached out to her cheek, and we found ourselves kissing. And then she pulled away for a second, looking a little nervous. I asked if everything was OK. She nodded.

I think I'm ready, she said, and stood up. I started to ask a question, but it stalled on my lips, as I thought I knew the answer, and didn't want to spoil the moment by guessing wrong. I stood up too, and she took my hand, and she led me to her bedroom. Vaguely, I wondered where her parents were, but they were rarely around in the early evening. She kissed me again, and then removed her T-shirt, revealing a pink bra underneath. I removed my T-shirt, too, and we embraced again.

We removed the rest of our clothes, and laid down on her bed, and kissed some more. I wasn't sure how long I should wait. I was thankful I carried a condom in my wallet out of sheer optimism. My hands cupped her breast, and she bit my shoulder, which startled me. She laughed, and I kissed her again, but then, after a minute, her whole body tensed.

I'm not ready, she said, pulling away, and I had no idea what to do. Suddenly, I was aware of my nakedness. I found myself just nodding. *OK*, I said. *OK*. I didn't know what else to say. I wanted to ask if it was something *I* did.

I thought I was, she said, apologetically. *I thought I was ready, but I'm not. Are you OK?*

I nodded. I didn't know how to answer. I was terrified that saying something would make the situation worse. I tried not to look at her naked body, which I'd been so captivated with mere moments before. With which I was *still* captivated.

I can go down on you, she said, with the air a waiter offers you free desert when your steak is underdone. It sounded like a consolation. I nodded, though, and tentatively, she wrapped her lips around my cock, her teeth clumsily biting harder than I think she intended The whole thing left me insensate, near paralyzed with pleasure. I couldn't do anything but moan, didn't even really notice when she'd switched from her mouth to her hand. It was over in minutes, and I pulled her close to hug her. I offered to return the favor, but she declined, instead sending me home with a kiss.

After that, we began to drift. She was suddenly less available to hang out, and we soon stopped practicing together. I kept saving money for prom, but began to wonder if I should even bother. Finally, she let me off the hook, saying *things were moving too fast*, and *she just wasn't ready*, and *can we still be friends?* My voice sounded robotic when I told her, *yes, of course, I understand*, and I don't think I spoke to anyone the rest of the day, simply biding time until I could go home, lock myself in my room and cry until I fell asleep.

She went to prom with someone else. After a couple half-hearted attempts to find a date, I gave up, and used the money I'd saved to buy an electric guitar.

Sixteen

There's a small closet just beyond our house's threshold, stuffed with old coats, many unworn for years. A few hung on a rack in our old apartment and haven't been worn since well before the move. Some have been added since, newly purchased and barely worn. And yet we hold onto all of them, as though they were laden with some untapped utility.

We both have light jackets reserved for cooler weather and rain. Hers are mostly earth tones. I favor basic black, although there's a light blue windjammer that calls to me sometimes on brisk spring mornings. There are jackets I don't recall my wife ever wearing. They may predate me by a bit. There is a yellow raincoat neither of us recall purchasing. It must have been left by a guest, but we have no idea who.

I have an old black trench coat back there, with '80s punk bands' logos pinned to the lapel – X, Agnostic Front, Stiff Little Fingers. It fits uncomfortably now, but I still love it. And I have a brown leather bomber jacket, the soft skin of the right arm shredded from when I took a hard fall on pavement one winter. I wore it for a while, rips and all, until my wife interceded. The newer black leather jacket – cut for overpriced hipster bars and not for pretending I can ride a motorcycle – is on a front hook, because I wear it often. But part of me can't throw out either the bomber jacket or trench coat. Too much history, I suppose. Perhaps I'm simply sentimental.

My wife's jackets see more use. In the back is an enveloping brown cloak with a hood that she bought at a Renaissance Faire for far too much money. It was colder than expected that day, and she liked the look of it. That was reason enough to splurge. For a time, she wore it everywhere, until some stoned idiot at a concert asked her in all seriousness if she was a druid, which annoyed her immensely. Amused, I pointed out that we actually *knew* a handful of Wiccans, some of whose company we actively enjoyed. She agreed, but reminded me that *they* don't dress up like *Dungeons & Dragons* characters. *They look like everybody else*, she said, and when I pointed out that they pretty much all have tattoos and piercings, she replied, *Yes! Like everybody else!*

I made a dumb joke about saving throws and hit points which made her laugh, but the damage had been done, and she stopped favoring the coat. She has warmer coats she'll wear in snow, but the cloak remains well-loved, albeit reserved for special occasions – the confluence of cold weather and old friends. To be perfectly honest, I've never really understood the objection. She's never been overly concerned with conformity or other people's opinions. Perhaps there was some hot button I couldn't perceive. Maybe it was just one of those things.

Every now and again we talk about throwing the old coats out, donating them to Goodwill or something, but somehow we never let them go. Maybe someday they'll be useful.

Seventeen

Sometimes, it's easy to understand the adulation of teenage love, how it's held up in pop songs and movies as the epitome of romance. Part of that is nostalgia, of course, a mistaken belief on the part of adults that it was somehow easier when they were young. Personally, I find marriage simpler, but I can see their point. Young love is pure bombast and opera. It begins and ends in a crash of percussion. Everything is new and vivid, every detail seems infused with *purpose*. Each date, each kiss, each awkward groping in the dark seems, at the time, monumentally important. And underneath it all lies the creeping kudzu fear that this thing is happening, and that it may never happen again. Somewhere, for many teenagers, is the fear that every kiss will be the last one. Until another comes along, and then another. But by that point, you're out of high school, on to college or whatever comes next, and your experience — whatever it was — has changed you.

For my part, I found young love to be a never-ending series of terrors: the terror of loneliness written on dark ceilings, the risk of embarrassment and ridicule. The terror of losing the first small, nascent love you've found. *Love*, we say, when we mean love, when we mean an endless cascade of questions one cannot answer any way but *yes*. *Yes*, when the strange girl kisses you out of nowhere. *Yes*, to pawing your best friend's girlfriend in a moment of weakness. *Yes*, to the blowjob from your teenage girlfriend, even though the moment is fraught with fear. Even though it feels like something is breaking.

Something is breaking. There is something inside you that *needs* to break, to understand the harm you can inflict on others, on yourself. Even if your actions are completely consensual, even if you have no wish to cause harm, you still have someone's heart in your hand, and it is more delicate than you have ever imagined, almost glass. One slip and it will shatter into a million shards. That never changes. Sometimes, if you're lucky, you learn to tread lighter. The early tempest of young love is where you learn that skill, if you learn it at all. Some never do.

What *lies* in the folklore, in the rom-com mythology of a million Disney fairy tales and prime-time television sitcoms, is the "Happily Ever After." Love that escapes the tempest of youth is rare, and in the end, is often much smaller than what comes afterward. Youth is a series of rapid changes, as you grow and learn and pull toward the adult you will become. We say *love*, but what we mean is often a fleeting happiness, an aria raised to the sky before the curtain falls.

Eighteen

The punk club where I hid from my adolescence resounded
with screams. The people on stage called it "singing," but their
fans held no such illusions. None of this was about beauty
and technical skill. This was about lit matches and kerosene.
Thankfully, it was all-ages.

I had taken to watching guitarists' hands, trying to pick apart
what they did, how they made the sounds they made, why their
music did or didn't work. I fixated on how some slid fingers from
fret to fret, plucking strings with precision, everything clean
and blue-sky clear. And then there were the others, the ones who
seemed to punish the guitar – bashing their hands against the
neck, tearing desperately at the instrument, cutting themselves
on nylon. Both schools had their appeal.

Every lonely child has a scream shoved deep into his stomach.
The loneliness congeals to nausea, becomes a seasickness, with
few tonics better than a license to release that scream. I spent my
childhood searching for a banshee's wail that never came. I didn't
know this was what I was doing, but it was nonetheless true.
I couldn't name the rumbling in my stomach until that scream
emerged.

By the time I was 14 I had a Rush poster on my bedroom wall.
"2112," of course. The one with the pentagram. In all honesty,
I had no appreciation yet for their songs' clockwork intricacy.
I was simply drawn to soaring power chords and ridiculously fast
percussion. And the lyrics: It was hard to pass up anything that
sounded like the soundtrack to a *Dungeons & Dragons* campaign.
The song *Subdivisions'* refrain – *be cool or be cast out* – hit close.
Rush spoke to my loneliness, but never assuaged it.

And then, there was the radio, and my secret fascination with love songs. And not just any love songs: The most mournful, brokenhearted tearjerkers I could find. Rush didn't really have many power ballads, so it was Howard Jones' *No One Is To Blame* Or Billy Joel's *An Innocent Man.* Or Phil Collins' *Against All Odds?* Oh, yes. There was something in that drippy, operatic devastation that resonated with my adolescent chest. Which is ridiculous, as I had *no idea* what it felt like to feel shattered after breaking up with someone. I had never been on a date at that point, never been kissed.

From junior high to about the age of 16, I think I was in love with every girl my age I knew. Not that I had any idea what love *was.* In retrospect, it was really just a wash of hormones, but I didn't know that. I only knew my skin's sudden tension when I saw them, the rapid-onset laryngitis when they spoke, the sputtering idiot I became in their presence. I wanted them – any of them – to touch me, but all I could turn to was desperate teenage masturbation and Phil Collins singles. When I was alone, I could croon along with him: *How could you just walk away from me/when all I can do is watch you leave.* I thought I wanted to have my heart broken. I had no idea what the fuck that meant.

Collins wrote most of the song that would become *Against All Odds* during songwriting sessions shortly after his first wife, Andrea Bertorelli, had left him. These were the sessions where he wrote the bulk of his most affecting songs, including *In the Air Tonight,* which would become the center of a veritable mythology: That it was addressed to a man Collins had seen watch someone drown, that that the musician had invited the man to a concert to hear him play it.

It's all apocrypha: Collins claims it was just glossolalia, spontaneous lyrics, more informed by Bertorelli's alleged affair than anything else. For some reason, urban legends cling to Collins, like the tabloid rumor that he divorced his second wife, Jill Tavelman, by FAX, which is likely a bald-faced lie. Indeed: The story sometimes mutates to have him divorcing his wife by FAX on an airplane between London and Philadelphia, when he was traveling to perform at both of the 1985 Live Aid concerts. But Collins had only been married to Tavelman for a year at that point, and they didn't divorce until 1996. Collins – whose original appeal was that he was a sort of average Joe – became something else entirely as people filled the negative space of him with supposition.

The punk club let me be anyone I wanted, but mostly I was just me. No Mohawk, no hair dye, no leather. Just jeans and a T-shirt. Sneakers. I didn't look like most everybody there, more Phil Collins than Sid Vicious. I looked like everybody *else*.

And who was everybody *else*? Is there some difference between the leather-clad punks with shaved heads and nose rings, and the frail, geeky boys listening to Rush at home on a Saturday night? Is there something that separates the goths in their black crushed velvet and the lonely burying their sorrows in sad Phil Collins songs? Aren't all of us trying to fill some space inside ourselves with alternating patterns of notes. We cling to these distinctions as though they're important, when the truth is the screams in our chests mostly all sound the same.

But I hadn't figured that out yet. I only knew that the club was the only place I felt at ease, and that the music there, the abrasive punk rock caterwaul, made me feel alive. I hadn't realized I'd been dead before, and was terrified that I'd be dead again as soon as the noise dissipated. In that terror, I clung to anything that made me aware of my own breathing.

Nineteen

I can listen to some of the schmaltz of my mother's youth now
– the songs that scratched at the base of my spine and drove me
to howling as a child. Some of them I've become quite fond of
– I love Roberta Flack's voice, how so much of its beauty floats
effortlessly in the air, unsupported by any melody or harmony.
I love the way Juice Newton can nestle the pinpoint moments of
heartbreak between phrases on *Break it To Me Gently*. I can listen
to James Taylor on a quiet morning, and feel something simmer.
None of them are my favorites, but I've grown to respect them.

There's no telling how much of that change is simply because
I've gotten older, and my relationship to that music has
transformed to something else. And there's no knowing how
much of the change is a distance between myself and those songs'
place in the cultural narrative, the ubiquitous chorus that tells
you what and how to love.

What are we when that chorus is silenced, when there is only
ourselves, alone with the song. What are we when we have no
need to defend what murmurs our heart, when there's no one
there to tell us that we're wrong?

Twenty

It is almost not worth mentioning losing my virginity. In the end, it was little more than the settling of a drunken bar bet my first year of college, a dare I was surprised she said *yes* to.
A dare I was surprised I was forward enough to make, although one supposes underage drinking helped facilitate matters. Other than that, it was unremarkable sex. The woman and I could barely speak to one another the next day, and rarely spoke ever again. I was beginning to feel this was a pattern. I wondered if this explosion of want and pleasure, followed by avoidance and silence, this shame that seemed to soak into skins, was normal. Is this the way it is for everybody? Is this the way it will always be?

Twenty-One

Writing a letter of recommendation for your office crush so she can get a job elsewhere is fraught with irony, worse because you know she'll get it. You can feel the lights of the sterile cubicle maze dim. It occurs to the villain in you to sabotage the application, say something cold or off-putting, insert diction that would make the reader feel she was *anything* but amazing. And the Junior Copywriter I've crushed on for years *is* amazing, not just for her easy smile or slender neck, the grace with which she moves or her soft, easy laugh, these things that arrest you when they hit you unprepared. In the end, you want her happy. You want to give her everything that she deserves. This is why you keep your silence.

There's no real space for this conversation, this unearned affection, no way to discuss both your heart, and how you have no need for action, reciprocation or change. You are happy in your marriage, as you presume she is in hers. And still you simmer, the avarice gnawing at you. *A little more than want,* you think. *A little less than love.*

I am certain that my wife is the only woman I have ever loved. This is my sun rising in the East, my inarguable fact. My marriage has been a lifeline for years, and I would not do anything to damage it. But of all the things it is, the only thing it *can't* be is *new.*

The letter writes itself. There is no denying the Junior Copywriter's supreme competence, the ease with which she navigates the intricacies of corporate life. They'd be foolish not to hire her, and I let the odd sense of preemptive loss wash away. I even count it as an honor to be asked to recommend her. It means ... I don't know what it means. It means that she trusts me to not say anything stupid. Which I suppose has been my goal all along: To not say anything to interrupt this stasis, to remain in her orbit, close enough to feel the heat of the sun, but not so close as to burn. It means that, on some level, I am on her mind, and that's a dangerous thought.

Both my wife and I have confessed feelings for other people
before. Strangely, it didn't damage us. The conversations became
footpaths through the wilderness of us, the fractal space where
we uncover new terrain of our relationship. Love is not a finite
country. Its boundaries expand and change as we change.
We uncover new niches and crevices within ourselves constantly,
the one aspect of old love that *can* be new.

Do I contradict myself? whispers Walt Whitman, from a poem I've
not read since college. *Very well then I contradict myself,*
(I am large, I contain multitudes.) We try to limit love's scope, drag
it down to an easily understood scale, when in truth, it's bigger
than that. It's bigger than everything. When we talk of love,
we mostly discuss a sliver of the thing, cells examined beneath
a microscope.

I have not yet mentioned the Junior Copywriter to my wife.
I probably will, eventually, but not straight away. From a certain
angle, that feels like lying to her, which is the one thing I try
to never do. I'd probably confess everything if there were any
small acknowledgment of my fondness, even the tiniest of sparks.
I've done so before, after all. But there hasn't been, and there's a
power in holding this attraction in silence, in letting the itch of
it fester unscratched. I wonder if giving voice to the crush would
dissipate it, if its power would wilt beneath the light of honesty.
There is a thrill in the lie of it all: *I could douse the flame any time I*
want, stop the blaze before it becomes a wildfire. One touch of her hand,
one kiss — if it happened, I could stop at that.

Energy can create or destroy. The honesty that fuels our
marriage could be toxic elsewhere. I try to remember this,
when truths better left unvoiced push at the back of my teeth.

The letter becomes a glowing recommendation. I hit send on the
email and sit quietly at my desk for a while, wondering how long
until this smoldering will fade, knowing from experience that —
for all my protestations — these flames never fully extinguish.

Twenty-Two

There is a dark-skinned man with kissable lips that works
somewhere in my office building. I pass him in the halls
sometimes, occasionally we share an elevator. He's older, with a
warm smile and kind eyes. I've seldom spoken to him, don't even
know his name, but every time I see him, I want to kiss him.
That's all. It's not an urge I have frequently with men,
but it crosses my mind occasionally, this sudden strange notion.
I would kiss this man, if given the opportunity, and I have no
idea what would happen next. Perhaps nothing, or perhaps what
often happens after a long-desired kiss, or maybe an alighting
of birds that squabble and squawk before crisscrossing the sky
in elaborate patterns before disappearing entirely. These are
the tiny, recurrent lusts, the unshakable ones which have no
other substance – no dreams of romance or marriage or high
seas piracy. There is a sleight woman with cat's eyeglasses that
frequents the same bar as I do, and I can't help but imagine her
fingernails clawing at my naked back. And there's a waitress
at a Chinese restaurant I visit regularly – I have flashes of us
fumbling with keys and belts in hotel hallways, not quite making
it to the rented room, blouses and shirts strewn behind us as we
grapple. These daydreams don't follow me home: This is just a
cursory inventory of the blood's small pulsings, odd observation
of what the particular chemistry of us evokes. It's the specificity
that interests me, the way the urge has no narrative before or
after that recurring tableaux. I suspect these daydreams are
eminently common, something primal that's always simmering
underneath our skin, but their constant-rerun pantomime
underscores a truth: That the fantasies that are more substantial,
the ones which may be love or may be simply water in cupped
hands, have a power to them that transcends mere autonomic
reflex, have a reality about them that's soaked into the bone.

Twenty-Three

The built-in bookcases in the living room sold us on the house. The '70s shag carpeting nearly drove us away. It was like a Carpenters' song from the '70s that my mother loved, but which drove me to howling.

Twenty-Four

Drunk and staggering, I found myself outside the bar, bracing for an imminent fistfight over a girl. Which was a new experience.

High school had ended in a flurry of exams and apathy, a sense of futility tainting every class or activity. Having already been accepted to college, I found myself pantomiming interest in the day-to-day, fully aware these things would soon dissipate into distant memory.

So, too, my relationships with people, as I became more and more detached. Sometimes I would just walk the halls, observing people's faces, wondering if I should commit them to memory, realizing that I would never see most of them again. Friendships forged at the club were a bit better — I suspected they'd be bound up forever in my love of music, and that world always seemed more real to me than school, anyway.

Still, it's hard to start anything when all you see around you are endings, and so I spent the purgatory summer disengaging, not pursuing dates or relationships, just playing guitar and getting ready to leave. Leaving seemed immense, almost incomprehensible. Everything was beginning to shrink — familiar places transformed to movie flats. People I saw nearly every day became extras. The summer made for boring cinema, but the reel was unwinding, nonetheless.

And so I arrived on an isolated campus near an unfamiliar town, with two suitcases, a Sony Walkman, two guitars and an amplifier to my name. The guitars made me strikingly visible, which was, of course, their job. As I unpacked bags in my tiny dorm room and greeted my biology major roommate, people drifted in from the hallway, drawn by the instruments, curious to know more about them, to know what music I listened to, what music I *played*.

Slowly, it occurred to me that I didn't know *anybody* at this place, which meant I could be whoever I wanted. With a little light cajoling, I grabbed the acoustic and played the only Grateful Dead song I like, *Friend of the Devil.* I chose it because it's a forgiving song — not terribly difficult, with vocals that lend themselves to an out-of-shape voice. Before that moment, I had rarely played in front of other people, and *singing* in front of other people was largely out of the question. This was new. *Everything* was new.

Soon, I wasn't quite the awkward kid I'd always been, found myself making friends faster than I ever had before. People liked hearing me play, and that surprised the hell out of me — it never occurred to me that anyone would be interested.

I registered as an English major, and took a full course load. Whenever possible, I explored — found the places where bands played, the bar which was a little lax about IDs. I had never drank alcohol before, but suddenly I found myself very interested. It was time to be someone else. I was discovering who that was.

The hippie girl and I shared several classes. She was an anachronism in the nascent '90s, her tie-die shirts and long, flowing skirts harkening back to an earlier era. There was a good deal of Neil Young and Jefferson Airplane playing on her boom box, interspersed with more modern favorites … some Red Hot Chili Peppers, a touch of Siouxsie Sioux. And I say, "girl," but she existed in a space where diction fails, she and I both suspended in a limbo between youth and adulthood, one foot in each. Do I call her a woman? I suppose so, but I would have been uncomfortable at that moment calling myself a man. She had an air of calm about her, a quiet intelligence that sparked in her eyes. I was a wreck pretending to adulthood. There was a self-destruct program engaged in my brain, toggling me toward meltdown. We were the same age. Could she be construed an adult where I could not? The question, and the underlying anxiety, picked at my brain.

We were in the same orbit, both English majors with mutual friends who only had casual knowledge of either of us. We drifted in and out of the same bars and clubs, although she seemed more sober at these outings and left earlier than I did. We smoked dope a few times with friends in the woods, but nothing remarkable happened. Somewhere in there, I lost my virginity, and it scarcely seemed to matter. The hippie girl, who seemed less and less a girl each day, remained on my mind, but I took no action.

One night, at the bar, a philosophy major — freshman, like us — was flirting with her mercilessly. We were sort of friends, and he was aware of my feelings. Indeed, it seemed everyone was aware but *her*, which is a little mortifying. He made jokes, and she laughed. He laid his hand on her arm as they watched some terrible rock band play. He whispered something in her ear, and that was enough for me. I excused myself to walk outside and bum a cigarette. I only really smoked when I was drinking, then, but I needed something to keep me from exploding, and I needed something to assuage the guilt of wanting to explode.

A few minutes later, the philosophy major staggered outside to find me, a look of entwined concern and annoyance on his face.

Alcohol blurs the exact content of the exchange — *you know how I feel* and *dude, you weren't doing anything about it* and *how could you* and *you don't own her* and other clichés we surely both pulled from some long-forgotten movie. And with each stumble-drunk parry, our bodies tightened, hands curling to fists. I hadn't been in a fight in *years*, not since the days of being sucker punched by bullies after school. I wasn't entirely sure what one *did* in a real fight, although I suspected the answer was *get your ass kicked.*

The moment slowed to a crawl, and I realized we were standing one one side of a Rubicon, each deciding whether to cross, knowing the next action wasn't completely up to us individually. I was breathing too heavy, and I felt a mild pinprick in my chest. Inexplicably, my cock felt tight against the crotch of my jeans, and that only heightened the terror.

But somehow, we hovered on that line, and instead of throwing punches, we found ourselves processing our emotions very loudly and aggressively at each other, as though we were in the midst of the world's most hostile therapy session. I cannot recall exactly what was said, but they were surely word-for-word transcriptions of some daytime TV talk show that we had both absorbed in our childhoods, but with all of the self-help garbage of the Phil Donahue era weaponized and pointed directly at each other. Seriously: There is nothing more pathetic than two drunk teenagers aggressively sharing their feelings at one another. The confrontation became an exercise in Mutually Assured Passive-Aggression.

The hippie girl, who had been observing this for at least a few minutes, finally had enough and stepped between us, swearing a blue streak — she decried our macho bullshit, such as it was, and our behaving like children. She reminded us that neither of us had any claim on her whatsoever, and informed us that we were both assholes.

She stormed off and, stunned, we both sat on the curb. He offered me a cigarette, which I accepted, and we sat quietly for a while. I could feel my body unwind with each drag.

That's some woman, he said, breaking the interminable silence. I nodded in agreement.

We really are *assholes*, I said, after a long pause. He nodded.

The cigarettes burned down as we both sat, absorbed in our thoughts.

Y'know, he said, breaking the silence again. *I play drums. We should start a band.*

Twenty-Five

At the time I met my wife, I was playing maybe four or five shows a month with three or four different bands. A punk band, a classic rock cover band, and a couple indie rock bands which I sat in with from time to time. They never really amounted to much — one of the indie bands had a label sniffing around, but nothing ever came of it. The classic rock band drew a good bar crowd, and that's how I made my living. That, and working in a record store. People always talk about wanting to hear original music, but they come out and pay money to hear what's familiar, karaoke versions of the Stones and Clapton. Not that I'm complaining. Like I said, it was a living.

Trying to make a long-distance relationship work was the stupidest thing either of us had ever done. I didn't even have ignorance as an excuse, as I had tried it once before and it dissolved in a matter of weeks. Still, we gave it a shot, and I incurred my roommates' wrath running up the phone bill. This was in the days before Skype and flat-rate cell phones. I was barely on the Internet. One of my roommates had a Prodigy account, but I really didn't know how it worked. Mid-20s, and I was already in danger of becoming a dinosaur.

Mostly, we traded mix tapes. She introduced me to Ani DiFranco and alt.-folk singers I was unfamiliar with. I sent her bands I was digging, along with old punk and ska she was unfamiliar with. We made a game of it, agreed that we weren't going to just send each other sappy love songs, but would instead try to tell each other something substantive about ourselves, through music.

Her First Tape to Me:

"Anticipate," by Ani DiFranco
"Round Here," by Counting Crows
"Scary Dog Man," by Pamela Means
"Prisoners of Their Hairdos," by Christine Lavin
"Dead End Street," by Jon Svetkey
"The Masochism Tango," by Tom Lehrer
"Is She Really Going Out with Him," by Joe Jackson
"Shipbuilding," by Elvis Costello
"The Ocean," by Dar Williams
"Little Earthquakes," by Tori Amos
"Conversation With a Ghost," by Ellis Paul

My First Tape to Her:

"Punk Rock Girl," by the Dead Milkmen
"Town Called Malice," by the Jam
"Godz," by the Clear
"Anything, Anything (I'll Give You)" by Dramarama
"Wild Sex in the Working Class" by Oingo Boingo
"Torn," by Ednaswap
"Waiting for the End of the World," by Elvis Costello
"Ever Fallen in Love (With Someone You Shouldn't've),"
    by the Buzzcocks
"Save It for Later," by the English Beat
"Little Conversations," by Concrete Blonde
"Ode to Boy," by Yaz
"I Would Die 4 U," by Prince

Putting Prince on the tape was a bit of a cheat on the whole "no love songs" deal, but *c'mon*. It's *Prince*. There's nothing sappy about it. And the Yaz song is just beautiful. I felt a touch of British New Wave lent me character. You think like that when you're young and in love.

This continued for weeks — random love notes posted across the country, arriving as fast as a first-class stamp would allow. We cornered ourselves into a pleasant limbo, and if I were completely honest, I would have happily lingered there longer. In the years following college, I had found myself in a rapid succession of dramatic relationships, and part of me was happy for the respite, the excuse to not pursue *anyone*, whereas I was afraid that if I were to poke at *this* nascent romance too hard, it would crumble like a saltine cracker. I was afraid this, like everything else I'd ever found, was only temporary … and that was a thought I couldn't bear.

My soon-to-be wife, however, was far more sensible and one day informed me she had bought a plane ticket and would be visiting. I was ecstatic, but also terrified I'd find a way to completely blow it. I convinced myself she would tire of me when she got to know me, that she would see me for the sham I sort of believed I was. I was a nervous wreck when her flight was delayed, and then delayed again, until finally, she emerged from the "arrivals" gate. I was almost tentative when I went to greet her, but she fell easily into my arms, and as I kissed her, I couldn't help but think it was as if we'd been doing this for years.

To be perfectly honest, we spent most of the next couple days in bed. Oh, I showed her some of my favorite haunts, and we went out to eat, but mostly, we made up for lost time, until the weekend dissolved, and I had to drive her back to the airport. The thought of her leaving was a cloud obscuring daylight, and I prayed for an excuse for her to stay, if only for one more day.

I don't know much about prayer, but my ancient, battered Toyota blew a tire on the freeway on our way to the airport. The tire exploded into plastic ribbons, and it took almost an hour for the tow truck to reach us. By the time we were back on the road, she had missed her flight entirely, and had to stay another day.

She kept a shred of the tire, to prove to her bosses she wasn't making up the story. A souvenir from the wreckage.

When she left for real, after a long kiss that ended too soon in the airport lobby, it occurred to me that I, too, was beginning to leave the wreckage behind. I wondered what mementos, if any, I would keep.

Twenty-Six

Now, after years away, I ghost through the street I grew up on, and feel nothing. Everything is the same, yet unrecognizable. The neighbors, both wretched and kind, have vanished, replaced by clones, identical in every way, save that I don't know them. There was a taco joint at the bottom of the hill, and a convenience store, but those have vanished, too, replaced by equally ubiquitous storefronts. The only thing familiar is the eyes of the lonely child, reflected back as I peer through windows.

What is left of us when we emerge from the wreckage, skin shredded by debris, bones splintered and cracked? When the action figures of yesterday are strewn across the yard, Batman's legs twisted off, Snake Eyes' arms broken, the Millennium Falcon lighter-scorched? When you have taken scissors to the comic books, rearranged them to create new collages: Spider-Man battling the Joker on the edge of space, Gwen Stacy plummeting to her doom, rescued at the last minute by Darkwing Duck? The baseball pristine in the closet, the basketball unbounced? Burnt-out shell of a television, transistors blown, outline of black and white images imprinted on the screen.

I had a dog, for a while, a brilliant shepherd who was my constant companion, until she died of natural causes when we were both 13. I held her as the veterinarian stuck her with a needle and put her to sleep. She was well-behaved, but had a howl on her when she wanted. You could hear it for blocks. Sometimes I think I hear her in the distance, still. Sometimes I think that howl is the only thing I've carried with me all this time.

Even the apartment I grew up in has been shuffled from the deck. I stand outside what I'm certain is the right building, but I can't even remember which window was ours. It's all too distant, and monotonous, all empty space I have no idea how to fill.

I have no maps for the place where I am now. My childhood was spent alone behind locked doors, and my family is drenched in death and divorce. Consequently, I have no models for what a marriage is supposed to look like. Each day married is, for me, uncharted territory.

I don't see this as a negative.

Twenty-Seven

This is love as shipwreck salvage, place where the word
"relationship" has tenuous meaning, where there are no promises,
only loneliness and drunken desperation, where we swear by
daylight there is nothing serious between us, that we're only
friends, and still we find ourselves at each other's dorm room
doors at 3 a.m., sleepless, burdened by the weight of night.

For a time, in college, I swallowed every lie I told myself,
digested them until I was sick. I told myself there was *nothing*
between us, a lie that buzzed in my ear as she fell to her bed,
as my teeth pulled at her panties, as her body quaked at my
tongue. And I told myself there was *something* between us, the lie
that stared silently at me from across the room as I shied away
from other chances at love, or sex, or happiness, or a moment's
peace between the darkness and sleep. And then there was the
final lie, the one that stared back at me from the bottom of beer
bottles ... that these were mutually exclusive feelings, that there
was no way these could both be true, when the simple truth was
this: I would rather have been lonely *with* her than anything
else without, that I was afraid to leave the shipwreck for fear of
drowning. The wreckage was the only thing I knew.

The buzz of contradictory lies made me deaf to the truth she
was telling me, that what was happening between us was all
she wanted it to be, that she was in no way waiting for me. She
told me point-blank that I was a simple salve to loneliness —
safe enough, undemanding — and I nodded, disbelieving all
the while. And when she mentioned other lovers who came and
went — handsome boys from the bar, a quiet woman who faded
in and out of her life — I choked down jealousy I knew I had no
right to, chased it with alcohol. I pretended that we were of one
mind, that the water slipping through our fingers was enough to
quench my thirst.

In retrospect, the woman in her life probably loved her more than anyone else, and more sincerely, and I suspect the opposite was also true. Still, there was something familiar in her eyes, the way she looked at her, the way she ached at being pushed and pulled out of her orbit, the way she chaffed at the stasis of it all. I recognized her want for *more*, and understood, just as I recognized that neither of us would ever have what we wanted.

One night, we found ourselves sitting together at the bar as the woman we were both not in a relationship with danced all night with a rough-hewn man we didn't know, and eventually left, her lithe frame hanging off his arm, auburn hair tousled, bangs fallen, obscuring her eyes .

Abandoned, we made small talk until our wallets emptied, and then shared a cab back to the dorms. Neither of us drunk enough for our mood, she mentioned she had a bottle of Scotch stashed in her room.

Two shots in, we confessed to each other the truth we already knew: that we were hung up on the same woman. Two more shots, and she jokingly suggested we should sleep together, to get her out of our systems. I reminded her she was a lesbian, and she simply laughed, until I was laughing, too. Two more shots, and she was on my lap, kissing me.

She was a tall woman, statuesque, with a beautiful face and short, cropped hair. I ran my hands across her breasts, and our clothing came off in an awkward fumble. She leaned down and pounced on my cock with alarming force, bopping her head up and down frantically as my body seized. For a moment, I lost myself in the roughness, in the four-alarm fire of it all, trying to decide whether I was actually enjoying this or not. It had never occurred to me that I might someday *not* enjoy a blowjob.

This was foreign territory to her. Briefly, perhaps out of empathy, I considered what it would be like to suck a dick, if I even *could*, but I was jolted from that thought by the force of her manhandling., which shocked me to sobriety. Then, I saw how tightly clenched her eyes were, realized she was clearly trying to get this over with quickly. I told her to stop, and pulled away. She was crying now, and I might have been, too. *It's OK*, I said, and pulled her close for a hug, kissing her gently on the forehead. We dressed hurriedly, then held each other until morning.

We remained friends until the end of school, and then lost touch, as sometimes happens, but we never spoke of that night again. I think she and the woman we were both hung up on *did* become more seriously involved at one point, but that was well after I'd begun to drift. I found I no longer wanted anything else from that quarter. *Amazing*, I thought, *how a heart can pivot to feeling little, almost nothing. Amazing how something so immense can simply vanish.*

Twenty-Eight

Nothing happened. We say this as though it were a final statement, as though the words had some palpable meaning. As if there is no truth in the proximity of bodies. It means *we didn't kiss* or *we didn't fuck* or *there was nothing between us but suspended breath and hands paralyzed with fear.*

How do you solve for the value of nothing? Is there some algebra that eliminates the variable of when she turns, and her dress swishes, and for a moment you are somewhere else entirely? When you and she are alone in an elevator, discussing stock projections or television shows, and in your mind's eye you see possibilities unfold? When you wonder, silently, if she is calculating the weight of nothing, too?

There are entire novels in the tilt of a pelvis, as the mind considers and rejects a thousand tiny sparks. *Nothing*, we say, but that word does not exist in the diction of our blood. We *want*, and are horrified by want, shove it down out of sight, let it rattle in the confines of our bones, cacophony that drowns out everything else.

That we succumb to this screaming is nothing remarkable. What's amazing is that we often *don't.*

Twenty-Nine

Some time after college, my best friend told the girl I was dating that there were two things she needed to know about me: That I didn't know what I wanted, and that I wanted to run. I couldn't disagree.

Thirty

A painting by my wife hangs in the tiny home office I keep at our house, the room where I write record and concert reviews for websites and magazines, where I sometimes just sit and read, or listen to scratchy recordings of songs on old albums, brooding on what the things of youth become.

The painting is a seascape — a turbulent ocean, rolling blues and splashes of whites battering a barren coastline. Waves crash mercilessly on jagged rocks, and in the distance, a boat rocks in the storm, perilously close to capsizing. She gave it to me shortly after our engagement. It's the sort of thing only she or I would think is romantic.

In the bottom right-hand corner is her signature, with her last name scratched out and replaced with mine. And then scratched out again, and replaced with her own. And once again, replaced with only a question mark. We've each shown the painting to a dozen-odd friends, and no one has ever commented on the signature, on the dithering over a name — that's not how they casually consume art, ferreting out the details and small paradoxes. They lose themselves in the roll of the ocean, the depths she captured in the midnight blue. The puzzle in the corner remains overlooked. Or perhaps the comments linger unspoken, too uncomfortable to voice.

It was no puzzle for me, though. She had dithered on whether she should take my name or not, so much so that she would work herself into fits of anxiety, once or twice even tears. For my part, I never thought it was a big decision — we never wanted children, and I saw it as an archaic custom, unnecessary in the modern world. I think, for a while at least, she doubted my commitment to that claim, or more precisely, doubted how sincere I was being with myself. There are things the brain can clearly see as true that the heart doesn't understand. There are irrational demons nipping at our thoughts all the time, emerging from the shadows of the mind where old, empty symbols still resonate — no custom that has survived that long, after all, is *entirely* powerless. Our tides are pulled by a thousand unseen forces of which we're barely consciously aware. No one knows this better than a painter. She saw the darkening skies before the wind picked up. She knew all weddings take place at the center of a storm. She was under no illusions.

In the end, the choice was obvious enough … she decided to keep her name. *I've grown attached to it,* she said, and I laughed, but I could see well enough the thousand facets of that decision, glinting behind her eyes like diamonds: How that name is a dozen signatures on the handful of paintings she had sold at that point, how it was embedded on her college diploma, hard-won on the back of years of work at fast-food restaurants; How it's emblazoned in the memory of whispers on old lovers' lips. And then there was the obvious truth, the Devil lurking in the custom's DNA: How she is not property, and has no desire to be marked as such. And the reverse was also true.

It took until well after I met her to realize how little agency I had ever taken in my relationships, how often I treated them like forces of nature, believing I had no control over where they went or how they ended. I was only ever any good at beginnings. Indeed, to this point, I have only ever ended a relationship once, and that was because it kept devolving to screams outside of bars and theaters — there was something in the way that woman and I interacted that was combustible, and it was worse because neither of us had ever been like that with anyone else. Not ever. With others, we'd both had failures and disagreements, moments of weakness and thoughtlessness, but never these sorts of eruptions.

I don't believe in the "psycho ex-girlfriend" — mostly, it's just a lazy interpretation of the unstable chemistry between two people, an excuse to absolve one's self of his side of the equation, an exercise in misogyny. The woman who brought this rage out in me, the pretty art student with her handmade love letters and stolen kisses in the cloakrooms of restaurants, was perfectly lovely, except when she was with *me*. And for all my faults, I don't think I was a terrible guy … except with *her*. In the end, I was the one who walked away. I was tired of being buffeted by wind, of constantly being exposed to the elements. I wanted to build something *with* someone, and I had no urge to control or be controlled.

This was what I wanted in a marriage. And this was what I found. And that, of course, in no way makes it easy. It simply means that when we look at the horizon, we see the same wind-tossed sea, waves crashing against the jagged shoreline. It is a storm we'll weather together. That commitment weighs more than any name.

Thirty-One

I finished out four years of college obsessed with impossible guitar chords and unavailable women. My particular fixation was "Layla," by Derek and the Dominos — the way Eric Clapton's and Duane Allman's guitars squealed, the notes entwining in the air as they soared at a breakneck pace. The song was originally recorded at 116 BPM, but Clapton later released it solo at 96 BPM — it was a version he could manage with a smaller touring band, but I always thought it took the bite out of the song. Still, I saw his point — my band could never pull it off at all , and after numerous failed rehearsals where it devolved into cacophony, we abandoned it from our set list.

When I went home for the summer, I briefly dated a dancer, but nothing came of it, save sudden, joyful kisses in the park. Finality tinged everything, and our attempts to keep things alive through correspondence derailed completely — one long, deep letter, and a reply. Then another, and a wait. And a reply. And then a wait. The letters became shorter, less personal. The space between them grew, until finally, it stopped. I don't recall which one of us sent the last letter. It might have been me, but really, it was an empty thing, devoid of all the good intentions we'd begun with. Sometimes absence *does* make the heart grow fonder, but mostly, absence is simply absence, especially when you're young, and your body is impatient.

Clapton allegedly wrote "Layla" for George Harrison's wife, Pattie Boyd, whom he was painfully, obsessively in love with. The title comes from the Persian story of "Layla and Majnun," about a man whose love for a woman burns so hot he's viewed by his village as a madman, causing his marriage proposal to be rejected by her father. In some versions of the story, he duels Layla's husband, and is killed, causing her to die of a heart attack. In other versions, he wanders the wilderness alone, howling poems into the sky, until he finally dies.

While I was writing letters that would vanish into sky, I began to see a woman a year my junior, a business major with straight-black hair hair and occasional haunted glances. We fooled ourselves into believing there was nothing between us — I was involved with a phantom, after all, and she had ghosts of her own — but our lips found each other in her room when her roommate was absent, shirts falling to the floor as we kissed until near dawn. She ended things the next day — said she didn't want to get involved with anybody — and I wrote my next letter, which had been neglected for weeks.

There is a flatness in my recollections. This time is a blur, pastiche of photographs careening through my mind, with no real emotional touchstone with which to connect. I ran into the dancer a few years back, at a coffeehouse, and didn't recognize her at first — this woman to whom I'd professed my love when she was safely out of reach. We spent an awkward 15 minutes not reminiscing: She talked of her daughter, and her recent divorce, I spoke of my wife, and of not playing guitar any longer. The conversation was negative space, illumination through what's unsaid.

Boyd eventually divorced Harrison and married Clapton, but both marriages ended in a flurry of adultery and substance abuse, or so the music press tells us. She's still alive, and has a successful career as a photographer, her work exhibited around the world. Our band broke up when I started dating the bassist's ex-girlfriend without asking him first, but that relationship ended quickly, too.

"Dating" and "relationship" might not even be the right words. Is there a word for two people filling the empty space inside themselves with sex, a simple phrase that encapsulates a series of unplanned fucks with no regard to consequence? Is there a word for willful obliviousness that causes chaos in the world around you, an unquenchable thirst that causes destruction but, ultimately, means nothing? Can we call it "youth" at 21 and "unforgivable" afterward? I wanted forgiveness and I wanted that band, but in the end both slipped through my fingers like dusk into twilight. The night the band called it quits, I tried playing Clapton's solo "Layla" again, but it moved too slow for me, whatever fire it had dwindled to embers.

And what's *really* sad is that the band never actually played a real gig.

Thirty-Two

This wreckage is what I've carried with me all this time, the rubble and splinters of the crumbled edifice I'd built to shield myself against ... what? I don't know. Maybe I built it as a child, the first stone lain when my father died, and then another at the first taunts of schoolyard bullies, and perhaps another when I first presented a card for subsidized school meals, the first weight of poverty. Maybe it was there from the start, branded in my DNA. I don't know. I only know it had always been there, these walls between myself and everyone else.

And this is how I tried to love amid the rumble, heart eroding like sandstone, drifting in the breeze, settling on someone's skin. Extended fingers only touching stone. Skin calcified while my insides dissolved. *A well-defined statue*, art critics would say, *but it has no soul.*

And even the carapace was flawed. One touch could reduce it to rubble. And I knew this, I think, which is why I avoided being touched in any real way, just drifted in the breeze from body to body, thinking only of myself. Trying to forget myself. Trying to assuage the omnipresent want, while always dimly aware of a fear of breaking, although something, somewhere desperately needed to break.

The woman who would become my wife cracked my shell with a single touch of my cheek, and all of the dust and rubble littered the carpet, the empty space inside replaced by love. And it is that love that binds me together, which keeps me from dissipating into air.

But I still carry the remnants of all that wreckage inside of me, and sometimes I can feel it rumble underneath its own weight. The debris of it all calls me. I lived inside it so long, it feels like home. And having learned to recognize love, I recognize there are women I never loved, no matter what I thought at the time, and there are women that I could have loved had the timing been different. And that thought hurts a bit, that ache of stillborn possibilities, and its in that hurt I hear the wreckage call to me, reminding me of all the nothing I was, all the absence which felt no pain. These are the lies whispered from the wreckage, the beautiful oblivion I once chased until I nearly disappeared.

Thirty-Three

When I first visited my wife's city, I fell flat on my ass. Unaccustomed to ice, I had no clothes to prepare me for a real December, and the soles of my shoes were gripless. Had never seen a blizzard before. Not really. Everything was new. I had to relearn how to walk.

The only things familiar were my acoustic guitar, brought with me as a sort of safety blanket, and her. It was really only the third time we'd spent any time together, and it already felt like I'd known her forever, knew she fit perfectly in my embrace. And yet, I knew very little about her. I knew she didn't like fish, but loved Vietnamese food. I knew she listened to New Wave when she was a teenager, but had mellowed into some of the alt.-folk stuff that was playing around. She liked live music, but didn't care for *loud*. I knew she got cold easily, and wore coats in weather where I'd just wear a long-sleeved shirt. I knew her paintings were usually abstract, but that she'd deviate into something more traditional if the mood struck her. I knew she didn't watch much television, and owned more books than I did. I knew she was left-handed, and fond of autumn colors. I knew where she wanted me to put my fingers and tongue. I knew she liked to be on top. In all honesty, I barely knew her at all.

And yet, here we were, in an ice-coated city that glistened in the frigid light, cloaked in the silence that comes when the cars stay off the road.

I wish you had come here when the weather was better, she said, and I just smiled and pulled her close. She squealed at the touch of my cold hands. I buried them in her sweater.

Far away, my record store job was waiting for me, as were the handful of bands with which I played. There were friends and family, familiar coffeehouses, beaches where I'd swum since childhood.

And nothing that can't survive without me, I thought, and I felt something shift in my mind, another in our marriage's cascade of beginnings. I blinked, and another recent college graduate took my place behind the counter at the record store, selling fewer and fewer vinyl records each day. The classic rock cover band put a flyer up in the back of the store, and had a new guitarist by the following Tuesday. The punk band disintegrated, but everyone agreed it was a long time coming. Nothing changed for the two indie bands I sat in with, other musicians stepping in as if nothing had happened. One signed to a tiny indie label, and did OK. The other eventually called it quits. My mother was upset, but understood. And after all, I had left before. The road would always, eventually, carry me home.

Home, I said aloud, not quite realizing I had spoken, and the woman who would one day be my wife looked up at me, quizzically. I smiled again, and pulled her closer.

I was just thinking it's nice to be home.

Thirty-Four

I say love is the fact of a person, what is inarguable between two people when everything else slides away.

Thirty-Five

The mohawked lead singer was spouting something about the military-industrial complex, but really, the crowd just wanted to mosh. I was OK with that, hopped up on Billy Zoom and X, trying to find a Zen in the cacophony, trying to transcend. I was seeking a punk rock Jesus, but all I could see was the writhing pit below the stage, the tightly wound aggression, the release.

The singer wanted us to be Bad Religion, wanted to write serious, political music. And on the whole, so did I … I wanted this hobby, this thing that had been a sideline my entire life, to take on some sort of meaning. But mostly, I just wanted to play. I wasn't as good as Billy Zoom, but I'd gotten better, and was finally comfortable playing in front of people. And with *this* band, it didn't matter if I was a little sloppy. We were … OK. Not *great*, but for some reason, we developed a following … serious college students clinging to a connection to punk rock that was probably tenuous when *I* was their age. They wanted political rhetoric they could dance to, and we obliged. And if we could keep the drummer sober until after the set was over, it would probably be a pretty good show. That happened about half the time.

I was barely a few years older than most of the crowd, but they already seemed so *young*. My own college experience had flown by in a flash of mediocre bands and only slightly better grades. Enough to walk with a diploma. Wasn't heartbroken when I returned home to figure out the rest of my life. When my last band broke up, I consciously stayed away from stepping into anything new, and when the last girl I'd been seeing eventually disappeared, I stayed away from dating, too. I spent my last six months in college building walls, trying not to form attachments. It was easier to leave that way.

One girl in my student housing complex — a cheerful young woman who talked constantly about her boyfriend back home in Iowa or Kansas or one of those places — sat on my bed as I packed the last boxes to be shipped after graduation. She'd had a few drinks, and was getting melancholy. She still had a year to go, but most of her friends were graduating. I'm not sure I was really one of her friends. I liked her well enough, but it's not like we hung out or anything. Still, she wanted someplace to sob drunkenly, and I didn't mind the company. Which surprised me, actually, as I'd been mostly keeping to myself.

She talked about loneliness as I struggled to make odd-sized books all fit in one square box. Somewhere, in the whiskey logic, she began talking about her boyfriend, and how she worried about spending so much time away from him, that she was afraid they'd grow apart.

You're just drunk, I said, surprised to discover that I was paying that close attention. *You'll feel better when you're home for the summer.*

Then she leaned over and tried to kiss me, but she was wobbly, and the kiss was wet and slobbery. For the next few seconds, we remained silent, as my mind weighed the possibilities. Finally, I sighed.

I'll walk you back to your room, I said, grabbing her gently by the arm and helping her to her feet.

You're such a nice guy, she said, but I just shook my head. I didn't really have a reply. She leaned on my shoulders as we shuffled awkwardly down the hall to her room. I knocked on her door, and her roommate answered — tired, disheveled. I could see her boyfriend looming in the living room behind her, and it occurred to me that both of them were graduating, too.

Sorry to interrupt, I said, trying to appear upbeat, *but I think this belongs to you.* The roommate, realizing how drunk her friend was, helped me slide her into the room and pour her into bed.

I figured I should bring her home before she got into trouble.

The roommate nodded.

Yeah, she said. *She starts making out with guys when she's had too much. Don't tell her I said that.*

I smiled, although a part of me felt a little less special at that moment.

Who doesn't? I said, smiling. *Her secret's safe with me.* I returned to my packing. I saw her in the distance periodically at graduation and at dinner, but we never spoke again. I threw everything I wasn't shipping into a car and drove home the next day.

Along the way I had learned that there are women who will kiss just to kiss, to feel a pulse of life within themselves. I had learned those kisses were not a promise of anything, and sometimes I could tell the difference. And sometimes I was all right with that. I had *wanted* the drunk girl in my room, certainly, in the casual way I wanted most of the women who surrounded me.

There is a moment, when I first see a woman, that I am instantly contemplating what she would be like in bed. It's an automatic function, I suspect a commonplace one, although no one seems to talk about in those terms. But she was pretty, with dark eyes eyes, and always seemed to be having fun. Except that night, I suppose, but then, she was *very* drunk. No, no good would have come of that, even though my sleepless night was filled with thoughts of her.

Billy Zoom plays in an almost trance-like state, as though he were deeply meditating on stage, his fingers flying over the fret board while his body remains placid, as though he were detached from his own music. He sports a grin while he plays, the whole experience radiating bliss.

My attempt to replicate that results more in me looking a bit sullen on stage, so much so that I was frequently mistaken for the bassist, who actually had a lot of funk in him and would jump on amplifiers to dance, reveling in his wireless bass.

I was always searching for ways to be steady amid the chaos, but also, I enjoyed being able to watch the crowd from stage, to see them dance with manic abandon, watch them fight at the bar, watch lovers entwine in the club's dark corners where they think they can't be seen. This is where I first glimpsed the art student, sitting back by the bar with friends. She looked out of place — clean, with a sharp pink skirt and a blue blouse. She was that sort of "girl next door" pretty that I'd come to regard as dangerous. She had curly red hair, bright green eyes. She was curvy, and there was a softness about her that gave her an appearance of youth, even though we were roughly the same age.

She was clearly at the club with her friends, who seemed to blend better, but then, she was a woman who stood out *anywhere*. She seemed comfortable, though, amid the ramshackle chaos. She seemed amused. I could tell all this in the length of a political diatribe against police brutality in roughly 4/4 time. She was gone before we finished breaking down our instruments.

Thirty-Six

The cinema tells us there's a narrative arc to dating when you're young: Meet cute, run into each other one or two more times, ask her out, go out two or three times, sleep together, become an item. From there, it either runs its course or you get married, depending on the sort of film you're watching. It almost never worked like that for me. In all honesty, during and right after college, I either ended up in bed with a woman on the first date, or there wasn't a second. There never seemed to be any in-between. Not for lack of trying: I took one woman to a concert, where we danced to Foghat all night. She kissed me goodnight on her doorstep, and I thought all was fine, but she was never interested in going out again. Or another woman, whom I'd long been lightly acquainted with, went with me to the movies, and then to a party, where we made out on the porch all night. But she was never interested in a second date, either. I assumed it had something to do with me. Perhaps they could perceive the wreckage that surrounded me, warning lights flashing *don't get too close.* Or maybe it had nothing to do with me. They were in the midst of their own stories, after all, not just bit players in mine. Sometimes, with the protective layers of marriage and decades between us, I'm tempted to track them down and ask what happened, but I don't know where to begin that conversation. Some I don't know how to find, or even entirely remember their names. And the rest are now casual connections on Facebook and Twitter, faces I see flip by on my computer screen, along with status updates about their marriages and children, about their jobs and scores on *Wordle.* Is there any way to look back and ask, *What happened? Why didn't we work?* Is there any way to breach that conversation without the appearance of wanting to rekindle something? Because really, I don't. I've already seen how those movies end. Perhaps it's best not to stage an autopsy of history, to dissect the details of small failings. And what if they *did* tell you, and there were apologies owed. Could I face long dormant culpability, a blame I never realized existed? This phantom looms larger than any sin I could have possibly unwittingly committed, begging questions: *What are you afraid of? How can you feel guilty for things you don't remember, things which may have never happened? Why is it best to not disturb the graves of stillborn love?*

Thirty-Seven

Someday, said my wife, back from dinner and drinks with her artist friend, *I'm probably going to have to just give in and make out with her in a broom closet or something. Is that OK?*

There really *isn't* a correct response.

Thirty-Eight

This is love as a repeating motif: The Girl Next Door is dangerous when she enters my life because she's always seeking demons I'm looking to *her* to exorcise. This may not be true for other people, but it's a cycle I locked myself inside for years, only barely comprehending what was happening, and why it never worked.

The art student vanished from my thoughts soon after she disappeared, another beautiful woman in a bar, simply passing through, stories never intersecting.

But I was wrong about that, as I learned three days later, when I arrived at the record store to find an envelope waiting for me … a handmade valentine, out of season in the early summer. The edges were stylishly distressed, and calligraphy swam between the margins, a beautiful ocean of words.

The note said she had enjoyed hearing me play the other night, and that she was hoping we could get together for coffee and talk about music. It left her phone number, and her name, I's dotted with hearts.

I remembered the woman at the back of the bar, but dismissed the thought. The odds of the only person who stood out that night writing me, a person whom I never spoke to, were astronomical. Still, a co-worker who was there when she dropped off the record told me she was a "cute redhead." Not a lot to go on, but I was intrigued. I called, and when she answered, I stammered though a brief conversation, somehow managing to arrange a meeting that night at a local coffeehouse.

Waiting amid the willfully eclectic bric-a-brac, I scanned the pages of the local alternative newspaper, not really reading anything, just something to occupy my mind, to drive away thoughts of how stupid this was, how I should really just run.

The panic subsided when the art student appeared in the doorway, greeted by instant hellos from people as she passed. It hadn't occurred to me that she might know people here, even though I suggested the place. It felt, suddenly, as though I were waiting for her in her living room, and the anxiety began to resume in small waves.

She beamed when she saw me, a "hello" I wasn't sure how to make replaced with a warm, oddly genuine hug. *I'm so happy you called*, she said, sliding into the seat across from me. *I know it was a little forward, but …*

I waved it away, *No, no. It's cool. It was just … surprising.*

Well, she said, *I don't want to be predictable.* She laughed when she said it, a full, natural laugh that seeped into your chest. Her manner struck me — there was never a moment where she seemed not at ease. I could have been an old college friend, as far as anyone watching was concerned. We could have known each other for years.

We talked about guitars. She had just started playing an acoustic — *only a hobby*, she said — and she wanted to pick my brain about music.

Ah, I said, trying to not appear visibly deflated, *you only want me for my mind.*

Well, she said. *I didn't say that.* We laughed, and I talked about Clapton and the Beatles, about punk rock and Joe Strummer. She was a practiced listener. She had a way of making you want to talk and talk, even if you normally preferred to let other people speak. She said she'd been trying to play songs she'd heard on the radio, and had gotten a few. I said I'd like to hear them sometime, and she smiled, and informed me she just lived down the street if I wanted to hear her play.

Speech abandoned me, and that voice telling me to *run* appeared again, hammering my words into a stutter. She didn't seem to notice, as I paid the bill and we sauntered down the street, as if nothing had happened. She talked the whole 15-minute walk, about how she had moved to the city from the suburbs, how she was studying painting, about her favorite artists and a trip she took to Paris for school the year before.

We got to her steps, and she fumbled with her keys for a moment before the door popped open. Before stepping in, she turned quickly, and leaned into my ear, *I could feel you watching me from the stage.* She smiled, pecked me on the cheek, and pivoted to enter, leaving the door open behind her.

Some moments are so perplexing, you have no choice but to just go with them, to follow the tide wherever it leads. Her apartment was small and spare, cluttered with painting supplies and easels. She had a couch in the living room, and a coffee table, but no television. She had disappeared into the small kitchenette, where I could hear the clang of a tea kettle and the hiss of burners.

She returned to the living room, and picked up a guitar that rested in the corner. I made myself comfortable on the couch, and she began to play the Fiona Apple song that had been popular at the moment, *Criminal.* Her voice was sweet, perhaps too sweet for the song, but watching her play was hypnotic.

The kettle boiled, and she stopped playing abruptly and scampered to the kitchen, returning with two tea cups.

You sounded great, I said, unsure how to continue the conversation. *You've got a really sweet voice.* She blushed, and sat next to me on the couch, sipping her tea. *I like that album it's on,* fumbling blind. *It's got a real edge to it.* She put down the tea cup, and simply smiled thinly. At a loss for words, I decide to kiss her, and it was the sweetest, most intoxicating kiss I had ever had. We embraced on the couch, kissing, for what seemed like an eternity. Finally, she broke away, and said, *I don't want to go all the way tonight, OK?* And I nodded, trying not to display disappointment. Then I followed her to the bedroom, where we lay kissing for hours, running our hands over each other's clothed bodies.

In the end, I left, wanting to honor her request and unsure of how far things would go if I stayed. We made plans for dinner the following night, and I sleepwalked home in a daze, head spinning.

Thirty-Nine

Winter gave way to spring, and I adjusted to the new city.
Had never lived with a woman before. There were whole new
rhythms to learn, minuets of bathroom rituals and morning
coffee, work schedules and dinner, electric bills and bank
statements. An adult life seeped into my frozen world like
the bloom of flowers — one flash of color, then another, then
suddenly, everything is green.

We took to sharing her car because I sold mine to pay for the
move. I took to dropping her off at work and then picking her up,
the purgatory between spent looking for a job, or noodling on
my guitar, or sitting in a coffeehouse trying to figure out what I
had done, the immensity of starting cold again, this time without
the structure of academia. There was nothing to fill my days
except searching, and no indication where to begin.

Applications at bookstores and record stores became a sort of
fruitless screaming into an empty void. I looked for flyers from
bands seeking guitarists, but couldn't find anything. I choked
down a disdain for working in food service to apply for waiting
jobs, but even they never called back.

Things were fine when she was home, although I think she
might have worried, too, that I was having so much trouble
adjusting, that college loan payments were eating the little
savings I'd accumulated, and that soon I'd be really and truly
broke. But was I *broken*? That question haunted me. I had
abandoned so much of what made me truly myself, so many of
the things with which I defined myself. I wasn't entirely sure
who I was, or at least, who I was in that context. I knew I had
never been more in love. But sometimes, when the day became a
wash of ticking clocks and coffee cups, I had never been so lonely.

The guitar would come out of its case for a couple hours every day, then a little less, and then some days not at all. It was difficult to see a point. The acoustic became my go-to guitar, and I found myself going back to the beginning, fumbling my way through old Beatles songs, straining through *Hey Jude* as my fingers struggled to relearn the melody. Amazing what I had already forgotten. Amazing how quickly you find yourself relearning everything you know.

Forty

Sex in the backseats of cars is rarely comfortable, the way it
forces the body to contort, the way exposure distracts you,
imagining phantom eyes watching in the distance.
It happened a few times, in the wasteland of youth, but always
from convenience. My bassist's ex-girlfriend, for example,
who I sat with talking for hours after a show, weeks after they'd
broken up. In those dark hours before sunrise, when it is only
two bodies and the night, all the reasons why you shouldn't do
something recede into shadow. We kissed, and our bodies twisted
at odd angles. She grabbed my cock and I hit my knees on the
dashboard. We fucked and strained our backs. And for those
moments at least, it was worth it.

The vulnerability intensifies everything, reduces the moment to
a pinprick in time, where there is no past or present. Each touch,
each thrust and moan — everything is vivid, and nothing else
is real. But the vulnerability picks at my insecurities, tears me
out of the moment. After a couple experiences, I was certain it
was something I didn't particularly care for. And as is always the
case, there is a part of my brain that wants the exact opposite,
that craves the danger, waves crashing on the breakwater of my
superego.

The art student met me at the record store, browsing through
old '70s soul music while I locked up and cashed out, before we
headed off to a dinner reservation. Springing for real restaurants
was a bit of a strain, but I was enjoying the normality of actually
dating, the healthy rhythm of it, the sense of *building*. She still
had a record player, and so when she expressed interest in old
Chic and Donna Summer albums, I put them on my tab as a gift.

She threw her arms around me and kissed me there, a forceful kiss — hungry, unrestrained. It lingered too long and my head began to swim. Her hands fumbled with my belt and she whispered in my ear, *Is anybody else going to show up?* I said no, but pointed out there was really nowhere in the store you weren't sort of visible through the windows, even though they were largely covered by posters. I felt Jimi Hendrix, John Lennon and Prince staring down at me as her fingers worked her way into my pants. I'm not sure if they were judging or approving.

Finally, and with much force of will, I stopped her. *We're going to miss our reservation,* I said, adding, *Later?* She harrumphed in exaggerated disappointment, but kissed me again and, after straightening our clothes, we headed off to dinner, where we ate pasta and drank wine. We laughed and held hands the entire walk home, stopping to peer in the windows of stores, imagining new lives together, ones where we could afford the things displayed.

She almost seemed bashful when we got to her apartment, and part of me wondered if maybe the moment had past, and I should simply kiss her goodnight and go home. But she invited me in, and within moments, we were making out on the couch.

Almost shyly, she led me to her bedroom, where we kissed again and I fidgeted to unbutton her blouse. We fell into the bed together, and I marveled at how beautiful her pale breasts were in the moonlight. Naked now, I kissed her lips, then neck, and down again, and again, and she curled her toes and dug her fingers into the mattress. But part of my brain noticed the difference between now and earlier in the record store, how she was willing but stiff, almost submissive, where in the store she was aggressive and forceful. She moaned, and I rose up to kiss her again, and we fucked slowly, almost mechanically, until she squeaked a tiny orgasm, and I came, and I held her in the darkness as she began to cry.

She apologized, said it was something that often happened after sex. She couldn't really control it. I'd heard of such a thing, but had never seen it in action. Still, a strange, creeping guilt crawled up my spine, although I couldn't figure out what it was I could have done.

Days lost to her school and my band practice, we talked on the phone but went a few days without seeing each other. Finally, we met for dinner, then took a walk along the beach. It was sunset, and the footpaths had mostly emptied, the tourists gone, and even the policemen and lifeguards vanished. We talked of trivial things as we walked, until we came to a lightly wooded grove that separated the beach on one side from the highway on the other. She stopped talking, and turned, the smile on her face saying everything.

We slipped inside the grove, where surly teenagers came at night to smoke dope and drink cheap beer, and she kissed me so forcefully I nearly fell over, riding up my shirt and biting my nipples. I was nearly paralyzed with entwined pleasure and fear, but she was doing all the work, so it almost didn't matter. I fell to the ground and she climbed on top of me, riding and thrusting until we both gasped so loudly that the fear of discovery took me out of the moment. I kissed her, and her face radiated joy, no tears at all.

I spent the night at her apartment that night, but we only slept. Eventually, the pattern became evident. Her, reserved and cold in the privacy of a bed; me, distracted and tentative when exposed. We went on like this for weeks, and more and more it caused a faultline between us, the tiny tremors of opposing needs rumbling louder, becoming earthquakes.

And part of me *wanted* to want what she wanted. There was a part of me that craved the thrill she reveled in, but it was a tiny voice in the cacophony of my head. The tensions became arguments, sometimes fights over nothing. Eventually the fights became screams, both of us in tears by the end. Sometimes afterward we'd fuck, but even then, one of us was always reluctant, depending on the setting. We were always out of synch.

To be clear: She was a lovely person, except with me. And for all my faults, I don't think I was that terrible. Except with her. It ended the day after our mutual frustrations devolved into a shouting match, and I left her apartment abruptly, staying up all night playing Nick Lowe songs on my guitar.

She came to the record store the next day, to apologize, but it really wasn't her fault. And as I looked her in the eyes, I knew it wasn't really *my* fault, either. *This isn't working*, I said, and her eyes welled with tears. But I think she knew it was true, too. We talked for a little while, and she kissed me gently on the lips, and then we vanished from each other's lives for a while.

We went on one more date, months later. I'd been seeing a rock star, and the whirlwind landed me devastated and crying in a coffeehouse parking lot, shattered beyond all recognition. I gave her a call, and we went to the movies. Nothing big. I walked her to her car, and we hugged and then, thoughtfully, she said, *I don't know if you were expecting anything, but it's not going to happen.* And then, kindly, she kissed me on the cheek and said. *You can't just repeat your past mistakes when things get hard. You need to learn from them and move on.* I nodded, and she smiled sadly, got in her car, and drove away. I never saw her again.

Forty-One

My wife and I both have rock stars in our past, talented
musicians with poise and presence, the sort of mystique that
captivates an audience before a single note is sung. She knew
hers from his early days, when she would see him play in local
clubs. I first saw mine across a crowded coffeehouse when I went
to see her play a solo set before my band was booked to open
for hers the following week. I watched her play and, for the first
time ever, I knew that I would sleep with her. Knew it as a cold
certainty, a fact.

It wasn't simply *want*, although I was captivated by the way her
dark hair fell across her face when she played, the way her smile
was thin and mischievous. It was something different, a strange
sort of clairvoyance where I could see the arc of a romance, and
it's inevitable tragic end. But I was still with the art student
then, so I choked down my precognition, although it strikes me,
in hindsight, how often the rock star was on my mind when the
art student and I were disintegrating. I can't help but wonder if
I had somehow sabotaged myself. The mind keeps secrets from
you. It doesn't tell you everything it knows.

My wife's rock star is a pretty nice guy. I've met him here and
there, over the years, even reviewed a couple of his shows. I liked
him, and liked his music, that Americana stuff that's everywhere
now, but at the time was still fairly novel. He was handsome, in a
Midwest farm boy sort of way, with eagle-sharp blue eyes.
I never found him threatening because nothing had happened
between him and my wife. And the few times my wife met *my*
rock star she was unthreatened because ... well ... because
nothing threatens her. My wife has the imperturbability of a
mountain. I have never detected a whiff of jealousy from her,
ever. My rock star tried to rattle her the first time they met,
at a party back home, but gave up and ended the night asleep on
the couch, with her head curled up on my wife's lap. *I guess the ex
approves*, said my wife, and I just shrugged and shook my head,
too amused for words.

I don't know the details of what happened between my wife and her rock star, but I know they orbited each other for years, and that the nothing that happened between them is pregnant with meaning and missed chances. I know there are things left unsaid between them, even now, and I'm at peace with that. That's a piece of her I have no business touching.

They drifted, for a while, and then became friends again, after a fashion. But still, she suffered under the weight of what was never spoken, wanted to find some way to have that conversation, to resolve the chord, exorcise the past.

We talked about it one night, and as we spoke I searched my heart for the specter of jealousy — which intellectually I assumed should be there — and couldn't find it. Instead, I just listened, and understood. I had too many things unspoken in my past *not* to. Leaving things unspoken creates a heaviness in your chest, tinges the color of everything that comes afterward. I got that. My head is filled with things I wished I'd said, but for me, it was far too late.

I feel like I'm giving you permission to have an affair, I joked, and her eyes flashed with seriousness, then lightened, a smile pulling at her cheeks. *I might have to call you from a motel parking lot and get permission,* she said, wickedly, and then, more seriously, adding, *But that's not what this is about.*

I get it, I said, and I did. We suffer in that silence, until the suffering has become such a part of our selves that we pretend it's always been there. That it doesn't hurt at all. It struck me, as we spoke, that what was important — at least, from *my* perspective — was *this* moment, and what we did with it. We had each other's hearts in our hands. They are more fragile than we'd ever imagined.

I'm OK with however it works out, I said, feeling as though I were watching myself speak from outside my body. *Just be honest afterward, and come home to me. I don't know how I'll feel, but I promise we'll work through it.*

We kissed in our kitchen then, and fucked that night until the darkness outside our windows was absolute, until we were the only things alive in the blackness of night.

In the end, it was all for nothing. Her rock star panicked when she emailed him, insisted there was nothing to talk about, and claimed that he barely knew her. Which was a lie, although possibly one he was telling himself. There were many miles between what they were and almost were, and what they were now. He had a wife, and a career, was protagonist in his own story, one where we were only bit players. Or maybe there *were* things left unsaid that terrified him. My wife showed me the emails. They were so obviously soaked in denial that anyone who didn't know either of them could tell what was happening.

We went away for the weekend, sat on a beach unfamiliar to me: Her barely speaking, me, struggling awkwardly to find a way to heal her broken heart.

Why is it that we can't just talk about these things, she asked me, after a silence that stretched for hours. I didn't have an answer. I still don't.

Forty-Two

The second band on the bill had come as a surprise. I'd turned up at the club to write a review of the headliner, a big indie rock band touring through, of which I was fond. I found that writing for music sites, even though it didn't pay much, assuaged the urge to perform, a commitment that just didn't fit well into my life anymore. Putting down the guitar was among the hardest things I'd ever done. There was no question of starting over.

I sat back at the bar for the first band, a bunch of local kids who were all right ... reminded me of myself when I was 20 ... playing sloppily, with passion. They had a crowd with them, also college age, and I felt a tinge of déjà vu as they sounded off itemized lists of all the things to which they were opposed. The college kids swayed to their easily digestible revolution ... same one I took three chords to 20 years ago. From this vantage, it was both endearing and a little disappointing.

But the second band ... that caught my attention. Three people on stage, one on mandolin, another on drums, and a young woman who bounced between keyboard, accordion and more with mad abandon, with a voice that sounded ripped from the distant past — a little Tin Pan Alley, a little Andrews Sisters, and then, in small, dramatic turns, a touch of Billie Holiday. I left my seat at the bar for the thin crowd to see better, early evening's college kids having left or gone outside to smoke. The vocalist held what crowd was left in her hand. And while I wouldn't necessarily have considered the music the band was playing to be, strictly speaking, rock 'n' roll, she was definitely a rock star.

To me, being a rock star has little to do with fame or even talent. It's that rare sort of musician for whom the act of performing seems to come as naturally as breath, who is so electric on a stage that an audience can't help but pay attention. This woman had it, a presence that belied her slender frame. She was beautiful, certainly, and wore a sundress that clung to her body, giving her every movement a subtle swish. But it was her voice, with its cascade of tones and shadings, that commanded attention. By a few songs in, I had moved to the front of the crowd, and soon I realized that she had that *other* great rock star gift: The ability to make someone feel as though she were singing directly to them. I knew it for what it was, but still, I lost my breath for a moment. It was only a reflex, but the body, sometimes, can be deeply stupid.

When the set ended, I drifted to the merch table at the back of the club to buy the band's CD. There was only someone from the club waiting there, minding their stuff until the band struck their instruments. The singer hurried back to the table, and I was surprised that no one else in the room was scurrying back after such a stellar show. The crowd had been thin, but they had clearly enjoyed what they heard. For the second time in the evening, I felt disappointed.

The singer and I talked the duration of the break between sets, wherein we chatted about her tour and I gushed awkwardly about her music. She smiled pleasantly and we talked easily, but I soon became aware of a thin wall appearing between us, and that *I* was the one building it. I became aware that I was very much trying not to appear to be hitting on her — I was, after all, a married man in his 40s, and she was a much younger woman who probably dealt with jerks all the time. My smile remained a smile, and not a leer. My hands fiddled with the newly purchased CD. I remembered where her eyes were. When the last band started, she told me it was nice to meet me and hugged me goodbye, and I made sure not to let that hug linger too long. I went back to the bar, ordered another beer, and tried to pay attention the headlining band, but I found they couldn't hold my attention at all.

I've noticed this reflexive reserve before, most commonly at work, the way I tamp down any hint of steam when dealing with women, the way I'm cautious to not inadvertently infer any sort of advance. It's not something I consciously do, it's simply a practiced mannerism. I often wonder how it's perceived, if the women I talk to, the ones I only have casual dealings with, can sense that artificial chill, if it makes me feel safer to talk to, or if the imposition of distance makes me somehow even less approachable. People can sense, after all, when someone is holding back some part of themselves. It makes them wonder what the person is hiding.

And sometimes, when I sense it happening, I wonder what I would find more frightening: If the woman mistook my intent and was interested, or if she perceived an advance and wasn't. Either are problematic. And still, whenever these thoughts occur, I hate myself a little. It's too reminiscent of my stumble-shy adolescence, the way my larynx would contract when talking to women, the way my vocabulary was devoured by fear. A part of me is repulsed to see even the tiniest shard of that painful shyness reappear, even if it comes from a different place. Even if it comes from an attempt to not be an asshole, and not the formless terror in which my youth was soaked.

I ask myself what it is I *want*, and get only silence in return. I swallow my self-loathing whole, push it back into the dark cellars of the brain. Listen to what's left of the music. Go home to my wife.

Forty-Three

The punk band wasn't particularly good, but it threw a great party. Maybe that was the secret of our success, but the bad news was, the party was always at my place. Well ... the bassist's place. He had inherited a house, and I rented a room from him to help cover the mortgage. For the most part, it was great ... he was kind of mellow when we were home alone, and we had a garage for the band to practice in. The parties, though, came often and sometimes without warning. It didn't matter if I wasn't feeling social — my bedroom somehow always became the cloakroom, my tiny bed buried underneath a pile of coats.

The art student and I had been broken up for more than a week, and I was feeling both more sane and miserable. I woke up missing the touch of her skin, the way her hair rubbed against my cheek when she fell asleep with her head on my chest. I missed her smile and I missed our awful, incompatible sex. I thought about calling her, but was resolute. The relationship wasn't doing either of us any good. Best to move on.

Mostly, I wanted to crawl into a cave, lick my wounds and heal. The bassist thought I needed a party to cheer me up. To be fair, he *also* thought we needed a party to celebrate paying off the cable bill. There was really no excuse too flimsy. Still, as the beer flowed, the living room chatter intensified and someone pulled out a guitar and started singing Violent Femmes songs off-key, I hid in my room, as best as I was able. People kept coming in and out, but mostly I sat in the chair at my rickety desk and tried to read a book.

That didn't really work, and by the time it became clear to me that I would have to crawl outside of my cave and be social, a petite young woman appeared in the doorway, taking off her leather jacket and tossing it on the bed before she even saw me. Noticing me there seemed to startle her, and she let out an uncertain, *Hey!* Which is what I guess you say when you don't know what to say. Most people who were dropping off their coats would see me, say, *hey* nonchalantly and then leave, but the girl lingered. *Whatcha doin'?*

I told her I was just reading, but I was going to head out to the party now that I had finished the chapter. Which was a bit of a lie — I'd been too distracted to get very far at all, but most people understand the urge to get to the end of a chapter before putting a book down. Or if they don't, I really don't want to know them. The girl asked what I was reading, and I told her as I lay the book on the desk and stood to leave. She didn't move.

The girl had been a fixture at a lot of our shows. I'd say "groupie," but I think she was actually at a few of the clubs before we were. We didn't really *have* groupies. We had people who hung out at our shows, and she was one of them, although when I looked at her then, I realized that she wasn't any older than 16. Maybe even 15. That made me a little self-conscious, even though I was about the same age when *I* started going to shows. I'd like to say that was different, but it really wasn't. Except I was never casually blocking the door of a guitarist's bedroom.

She made small talk while I remained impassive, projecting an aura of casual obliviousness. It is the only stereotypical male self-defense mechanism in my arsenal — I can do it now, on a dime. She mentioned she was single at least twice. I nodded, and tried not to look at how tightly her Metallica T-shirt clung to her chest, but I can't guarantee I succeeded. Her clothes hugged her body, jeans seemingly spray-painted onto her legs. She played with her hair as she talked.

Silently, I pleaded for someone to come into the room and drop off a coat, but it didn't happen. It's not that the girl wasn't attractive — quite the opposite — but there was something dangerous in the air, even more than just her age. She reminded me, in some ways, of my first girlfriend, back in high school, with her tiny frame and air of cool. But I also remembered the night we almost lost our virginities. Or maybe *did* lose them. Neither of us emerged from that awkward night unchanged.

I remember her resolution, how she was determined to have sex that night, and it strikes me that I never asked what brought her to that decision, why she was suddenly so determined when, in hindsight, she clearly wasn't ready, and didn't even really *want* it. And then, I remembered that blowjob, my first, and how the world seemed to shatter around us. Isn't *that* losing your virginity, in every way that matters … when the weight and reality of sex crashes around you, teaching you things that you can never not know again?

The girl stepped closer to me. I excused myself and stepped around her, leaving her behind me. She followed me out the door, but returned to the party in the living room, while I headed to the kitchen for a drink.

The rock star was there with a bottle of Jack Daniels. I could see her eyes follow the trail from my room, to the girl now chatting in her sight lines across the house.

Something happen between you two? she asked, more curious than accusatory. I shook my head and sighed. Her eyes seemed to dissect me for a moment, and then she nodded in understanding, and poured me a glass of whiskey.

Forty-Four

The college loan payments flew unfettered from my wallet. My
soon-to-be wife was nice about my not splitting the rent until
I got a job, but even her patience was beginning to fray. I threw
money at her for the groceries, but that only helped a little.
I read the newspaper want ads, but they all seemed written in
some strange hieroglyphics, any path forward they might offer
obscured and indecipherable. I tried looking for gigs, but no
one knew who I was, and I couldn't find a band anywhere that
needed a guitarist. There is a way uselessness burns at a man. It
was consuming the lining of my stomach. It's aftertaste tainted
everything I ate.

Is love enough when every other thing that makes you what
you are disintegrates? More than once, it occurred to me that
I should just go home and start over again. I had friends that
would take me back, with only a modicum of ribbing. There were
bands that knew me, and I'd find a permanent place with one of
them again. Or I could form a new band. I knew enough people.
It wouldn't be hard. These thoughts picked at my brain while
I was home alone, until I couldn't take them anymore and headed
out to distract myself.

And in my head, as I walked to the coffeehouse to be alone in
public, I heard the art student's voice: *You can't just repeat your
past mistakes when things get hard.* I wondered which had been the
mistake — leaving home or staying here — until my someday-
wife came home from work and we talked about nothing on the
couch, and I had my answer. I knew I wanted this life, and I
didn't want to run away from it. And in that realization, I didn't
even recognize myself.

I took to playing cover songs at an open mic, and although
I realized that I was really not that interesting a musician outside
of a band, it helped ease the sense of uselessness that creaked in
my bones. No gigs came from it, but I began to know the local
scene a little. And one day, waiting for the show to start,
I thumbed through the local alt.-weekly to see if any good bands
were coming up, and had an epiphany. The next day, I called
the office, and spoke to the editor. I told him I didn't have any
experience, but I knew music, and I'd write for him for two
months as an "intern." He thought about it, and asked me to
review a local folk musician playing across town that week, and if
he liked that, we had a deal.

A week later, my review had been chopped down to a capsule,
but it made the paper. I was given a spare desk back by the filing
cabinets, and article by article, review by review, I was taught
how to write my own future.

Forty-Five

What does it mean to change, to transform one's self from being one thing to being another? You can change what you *do*. You can quit smoking, pick up a needle, vote Republican, sit in church pews every Sunday until you believe the words through rote repetition. You can take up yoga, learn to love football, take night classes to become a dental hygienist. You can go vegan, drink only whiskey or develop a fondness for running, or blackjack, or internet pornography. You can drink until you're blind and go home with strangers, go online and find someone to whip you 'til you beg, stay home and tend your garden on lonely Saturdays. You can pick up a guitar, and everything around you will change. Or you can pick up a guitar, and nothing will change at all. You will still be that gawky kid whose appropriately trendy clothes no longer camouflage him, standing slack-jawed as the band thunders on in two-and-a-half chords and truth enough for another song.

Does love change you? Does marriage? Does the fact of a person in your life change the way you react, new data in the system, acknowledgment of new parameters? Or do you do that yourself, transform cell by cell, replace skin with skin, and bone with bone in a million small surgeries, spread out over decades, until you are no longer the person you were. Until there is a stranger staring back at you in the mirror, and that other person you were seems distant and odd, strange movie you saw as a child, half-asleep on the couch, up past bedtime.

Here is the truth: You will change because you change, because your muscles have a memory, carry the pain inflicted on you forever; the pain you've inflicted on yourself. And you will hurt yourself until you find some way to make that stop, and maybe love will be that thing you cling to as you extract yourself from the mire. Or maybe you will remember the pain you've caused to other people and try to stop inflicting it. And maybe *that's* a kind of love, also. Or maybe you'll not learn a single thing, repeat yourself again and again until the body count is undeniable, until the house is already burning. Until even the air itself is ash. There is only your relationship to love, and pain, and what you choose to do with them. There is only the decision of what air you choose to breathe.

Forty-Six

It's rare, these days, for me to be alone. I'm not fond of going out without my wife, and am often ill at ease when she's not there, like I have to apologize for her absence. It's like trying to quit smoking: It makes me anxious, I forget what to do with my hands.

It's even more rare for my wife to be out of town without me, but once in a while a graphic design client needs her on site for meetings in some distant city, and I ward off the encroaching silence with pizza and *Doctor Who* reruns. Sometimes the guitar comes out of the closet when she's gone, but only sometimes. It depends on my mood, on how poorly I'm adjusting to the quiet.

When a friend from out of town called and asked if she could crash at our place, I welcomed the company. She was flying in late, and didn't want to wake her parents, who lived a couple hours away, by showing up in the middle of the night.

She was one of the first friends we made as a couple. We often went out for dinner with her and her husband, but even then the frays between them were obvious — they were far too quick to spend time apart, and even if they never quarreled publicly, there was an easily perceived aura of unhappiness that surrounded them. Their divorce surprised no one, but my wife and I were both saddened that she took a job in Chicago afterward. She had become a part of our lives, and the sense of loss was as palpable as it was selfish.

Single life had suited her. She had always had a girlish air about her, a youthful face that belied an indelibly adult manner, but when she arrived on my doorstep, she seemed younger than ever. There was a brightness in her eyes that had dimmed in the months before she finally left. We hugged, and I hefted her bags up the stairs. I ordered pizza, and she told me about her new life, and then, when the pizza arrived, we talked about poetry.

She was one of the best writers I knew, and did absolutely nothing with it. Poets were a dime a dozen on the periphery of the music scene, and while some were excellent, most were either boring or garbage. She filled notebooks with the stuff, much of it fantastic, but declined to send it out or read it in public, quoting Robert Heinlein back at me when I suggested she do so. *Poets who read their work in public might have other bad habits.* She would show it to friends, but insisted that she only wrote it for herself. I could respect that, even if I disagreed.

But we talked, and I grabbed a bottle of wine from the kitchen cabinet and she read some poems. And then, tired, she put the poems away and we wound down the evening watching television.

Somewhere along the way, I became someone who knew a lot of people but had few close friends. That wall of reserve, that imposition of distance often prevents me from getting too close to people. But this woman was *truly* a friend, and what's more, I'd been at ease around her from the beginning, since my wife and I met her at a coffeehouse folk concert. And nowhere was that casualness more in evidence than that night, tipsy with wine, leaning on opposite ends of the couch, her feet propped up onto my lap.

Science fiction characters blurred on the screen — time travel and aliens and rather a lot of running, delivered between quips. Without thinking, I began to rub our friend's feet, and she purred. It didn't occur to me immediately, but it was the most intimate I'd been with a woman who wasn't my wife in years. My body had forgotten the electricity that comes the first time skin touches skin. I glanced at her face, and noticed she was looking at me out the corner of her eye, still smiling pleasantly. Our eyes, near in unison, flicked back to the television, until a commercial appeared and, absently, a Rolling Stones song played in my head. *But he can't be a man 'cause he doesn't smoke ... the same cigarettes as me ...*

Casually, she curled her body upright on the couch, then leaned over and hugged me. *It's been a long night*, she said, and stood. *I should get to bed.* I concurred and told her where the coffee and cereal was if she woke up before me, told her to help herself.

Unable to sleep, I read for a while until I couldn't see the words anymore, until I re-read the same sentences over and over, unable to retain them. I turned off the light, but still didn't fall asleep. I stared at the darkness, then blinked, and she was straddling me, breasts hanging beneath a loose T-shirt, hair falling forward, covering her eyes, a serious smile on her face. I could feel her body on top of mine, feel her breath on my cheek. And then I blinked again, and she was never there, and sleep seemed further away than ever, although it must have come eventually, because I awoke to sunlight on my face, unsure of when I had drifted off.

In the kitchen, there was coffee in the coffee maker, and a cup in the sink, along with a note thanking me for letting her stay, explaining she woke up early and wanted to get going to her parents' house. The coffee was cold, despite the thermal carafe, so she must have left hours before. We spoke later that evening, and it was pleasant and friendly, and we've seen each other since, many times, and it's always as if nothing had changed.

But something had shifted in my blood, and I had no idea what to do about it, if anything. There was a silence welling in my chest, monster beneath the surface of the lake, waiting to break the surface, And all the while, Mick Jagger's voice echoed in my head, *I can't get no ... oh, no, no, no ...*

Forty-Seven

I had always intended to sleep with the rock star and hated myself a little for thinking of it that way. Had never been a man who marked sex on a scorecard, but still, it's impossible to deny that there are women I want to fuck just to fuck them. Even if I don't pursue the urge. Even if the idea seems so distant and impossible as to not even rise to real want, a mere abstraction of desire.

What's worse, when I was young and single, these were the easiest relationships to chase ... the ones which were, at first at least, purely physical. These were the circumstances where my voice didn't crack, where I could simply let the tide pull me. Things happened, or they didn't happen, and I was fine.

Except I *wasn't* fine, and I knew it. Loneliness frosted my heart, left me shivering and shaking alone in the night. There was a cold settling in my bones that terrified me, made me more somnambulist than anything. I'm aware of what that cost me.

The rock star and I spent the whole party in the kitchen talking music and drinking whiskey. She was impossibly thin, with tight leather pants and a P.J. Harvey T-shirt. She was at least five years older than me, maybe more, but I found that interesting, liked that she was a woman, not a girl. The teenager in the other room had rattled me, and the art student was still always on the periphery of my thoughts. As bad as things had gotten with her, I found that I enjoyed being in an actual relationship, and was tired of being driftwood, tired of sleepwalking. I wanted to wake up. I wanted to be alive.

The whiskey didn't seem to slow the rock star down at all, and as she rattled off the finer points of bands like the Runaways and X-Ray Spex, I felt that strange certainty again, the bone-deep knowledge that we'd sleep together. *That* feeling unnerved me. Having never encountered that sort of clairvoyance before, I thought for certain it was wishful thinking. The clock ticked past 1 a.m., and almost everyone had gone, and we had finished the bottle. She was sober enough to know she was too drunk to drive. I offered her my room, told her I would sleep on the couch. She told me there would be drunks on the couch until dawn, took my hand, and led me to my own bed. I shut the door behind me and we kissed and fumbled with each other's clothes. We fell on the mattress and fucked loudly, manically, as if the morning would never come.

Forty-Eight

It might have been different if we'd had children, but we never wanted any. She had her own reasons and — I would have told you at the time — I needed to concentrate on my music, which was true enough. But the real truth was that I was terrified of the loneliness that blanketed my *own* childhood, and I couldn't bear to see that reflected anywhere, couldn't face the possibility of passing it on. I wanted that loneliness to die with me.

And what now, when the calluses on my fingers have healed, when I can't fingerpick without drawing blood? I work in an office, shuffling paper and returning email. I have become an observer to the catechism of song, watching distantly from the pews. The time I thought I'd spend creating art has slipped through my fingers, sacrificed on this altar of adulthood. The cultural narrative tells me I should harbor regrets, but I have none, feel no responsibility to hypothetical children, agree they might have added joy and purpose to the hollow spots in my chest, but feel no need to change. Even if I can never banish the aching restlessness from my blood, I know I am as content as I could ever be. I don't think having children would change that — I have seen fathers who are not content, who let the restlessness overwhelm them, until they are gunpowder, awaiting sparks. I have seen the debris they leave in their wake.

There is no formula for how to be an adult, how to be a man. I am who I am because of the choices I have made, because of the times I have been reduced to shattered glass, and the times love has patched me back together. Call me a patchwork man. Say that we *all* are. I sacrificed one future filled with family and children for one filled with music, and do not regret that. Then I traded that future for one filled with love, and do not regret that either. There is no *one* right path, although probably several *wrong* ones. My decisions were as right as they could be, as right as anyone's could be.
I do not mourn what I never had, even if sometimes, when I peer out the kitchen window at the traffic in the distance, I see all the places the highway could have led, and feel a wistfulness, a nagging question that itches under my skin.

Forty-Nine

Nothing happened, but I couldn't deny it was the sort of nothing that had mass, a nothingness that presses on your shoulders and chest. This is the heart as deep-sea diver, swum so far down it doesn't know which way is up, surfaced too fast and aching from the change in pressure.

Outside the airport, I smoked a cigarette and watched tired people leave the terminal, dragging suitcases. Some fell into someone's arms immediately, some hailed a taxi, some walked toward the parking structure, where a car was presumably waiting for them. Some were probably visitors, but many were coming home from somewhere, with all the good and bad returning to one's real life entails.

I could see my wife enter the baggage claim through the window. I stubbed out my cigarette and shuffled inside to greet her. We kissed, then hugged, and since she was smart and only brought a carry on, we left. I asked her how the job went, and she regaled me with the tedium of office work, gleefully proclaiming how there was no real reason to have her there at all, but that the hotel was nice. She had stolen soap as a memento.

She asked me how I had spent my time, and I recapped the plots of television shows she had mostly seen the first time. And then she asked me about our friend visiting, and how that went, and I think my heart skipped a beat. Guilt clawed at my esophagus, which was annoying since nothing had happened, and I had nothing to feel guilty for. Except *feeling*, I suppose, but how was I supposed to control *that*?

Fine, I answered, glad for the excuse to watch the road and not look her directly in the eyes. *She's OK. She's ...* and then, I pondered the truth, as ephemeral as any truth was to be had in the matter. And I considered saving this conversation for when we weren't on the freeway, but here it was in front of me, and I didn't see any exit without lying. Maybe the smallest of lies, but lies nonetheless.

I'd lied by omission in our marriage before — had once concealed the rising tide of debt, how much difficulty I was having paying bills. I pretended things were fine until I couldn't any longer, and the conversations that followed were ... difficult. And I felt better afterward, and we began clawing away at our problems *together*, which made them bearable. But I had learned a lesson about silences, about the way they pool in your stomach, until they make you sick. Even years later, I could taste the bile they left in my mouth.

Look, I said. *I need to tell you something. Nothing happened, but ...* and I faltered for words, trying to wrap my tongue around the empty weight. *There was a moment when ... ... there was a moment on the couch, and ...*

My wife searched my face for the words I was failing to conjure. I watched the road and stammered.

You sparked? she offered, cautiously, imbuing the word with no portent. It hung there in the car as I drove.

Yeah, I said, finally, relieved to have a name to hang it all on. *Nothing happened*, I repeated. *Not even close, but still ...*

Hey, she said, sensing my discomfort, honeying her words. *It's OK. I'm glad you told me.*

We talked easily then, as though discussing the grocery list or plans for Thanksgiving. I told her how the feeling came out of nowhere, and reiterated that I didn't act on it. I didn't go so far as to recount my fleeting dream that night ... that seemed a bridge too far ... but otherwise I left nothing out. I told her I didn't know if she had felt the same, but suspected she might. She asked me if I was in love with her, and I responded as honestly as I could: *I don't think so, but I could be if I let myself.*

She asked me if I was going to talk to her, and I said *no*, explaining that I didn't feel I had the right to impose myself in her life like that, and that I didn't want to hurt either of them, or myself, or anyone.

What could I offer, I said, with all the honesty I could muster. *I don't just want to sleep with her, and any relationship would be ...* I fumbled for the word ... *secondary ... to our marriage. How could I ask that of anybody, especially someone I care about?*

My wife smiled, leaned back in her car seat, and glanced out the window at the manicured trees lining the freeway. She put her hand on my arm.

See, she said, chuckling a bit. *That's why I'm glad I'm married to you. Other people are tricky.*

Fifty

It was months until the rock star admitted we were in a relationship, months where I slept mostly in her bed; months of late dinners after shows, months of settling into a comfortable routine. She conceded one morning, after fucking in the shower, that whatever was between us was more than just sex. That sort of moment brings out the honesty in people, that collision of vulnerability and cleanliness — facades slide off like soap.

Our love was leftover pizza and musical arguments. Not that we called it love. Not that we called it *anything* for a long time — me, unaccustomed to stability, she unused to tenderness. She trailed a string of dangerous boys behind her, all laid low and shattered, save perhaps the ones that hurt her first. And beneath that something darker still, a wound whose existence I only learned through inference. She slept with the bathroom light on, enough illumination that her bedroom was never completely swallowed in night. I sensed enough to not probe too deeply, enough to let her demons lay dormant.

If I ever loved anyone before I met my wife, it was her: Her fondness for black coffee and good latkes; her snobbish taste in beer; her penchant for losing herself for hours on end in Janis Joplin records, vinyl still; her peculiarly detailed accounting. She was not so successful yet as to support herself entirely through performing — taught music lessons, acted as a voice coach, did some studio work on some big label releases. She existed in that purgatory between the strictly local musician and the nebulous larger world beyond that, the one that glitters on the periphery of vision, unattainable Avalon for most. She could almost touch it.

I was playing with multiple bands, usually two, sometimes as many as four. She just had the one, but often played three or four times a week, including some solo gigs. Sometimes we'd go days without seeing each other, or we'd collude like thieves in the night, stealing moments between the breakdown and the morning. Her voice was honey-tinged whiskey. There was a bite when she sang. You could feel her songs in your skin. I never played with her band. Always thought it was out of my league. She chided me for my lack of ambition. One night, at a party to commemorate a burnt-out amplifier, my bassist roommate told her there were only two things she needed to know about me: That I don't know what I want, and that I want to run. He confessed saying this early the next morning, when the gin had worn off, but I had no real reply, knew I had carved a comfortable stasis. Knew how it would end.

Fifty-One

There has always been a live viper-nestled in the recesses of my heart, hidden so deep I only knew of its existence when it bared its fangs.

Fifty-Two

How much of what we dress as nobility is simply a scarecrow, wisps of fear flocking around our head like starving birds, molting black feathers falling around us like rain?

I skip my office crush's going away party, because I'm terrified to say goodbye. Instead, I catch her at her desk, wish her well, and excuse myself back to the safety of my cubicle, to the never-ending series of pointless tasks that await me there. *Does she know how I feel*, I wonder, then disregard the question. How *could* she, when even I can't sort the answer out? I hide in silence, and pretend it's simple decency. I am unsure how well the mask I've constructed disguises me.

Of course you like her, says my wife, after three Manhattans and a jazz concert have pried open my lips on the subject, *she's smart and she's got a great rack*. I laugh, an honest, bourbon-freed laugh that wells from the pit of my stomach. It's the kind of laugh that can only come when the suffering of silence is alleviated, when I am in that space with her, and we can be honest, without fear of judgment. If anything, I think she likes these moments of earnestness, think she might enjoy standing beside me so close to that fire, but I never pursue that thought too deeply.

She confesses few crushes, mostly odd TV personalities: character actors on favorite TV shows, a blonde, British improv comic with cute glasses and a sharp wit we discovered on YouTube, maybe Chris Hemsworth, but let's face it, that's true of everybody. Sometimes she talks about the friend who's been smoldering quietly around her for years, the artist whose heat she's confessed to occasionally reciprocating. But she's folded that desire away, for the moment, unwilling to deal with complications, to damage friendships. Another drink, and she confesses she's doesn't like the way she is with women: too mannish, too aggressive.

Part of me would actually like to see that for myself, but it's not the sort of thing you push too far. Besides, there have been women who brought out sides in me I didn't care to see, so I can relate. At least a bit. And it doesn't escape me that I'm somewhat submissive in bed with her, that I let her initiate sex, that I prefer to be beneath her, finding joy in surrender.

It is only in the ocean of her that I am completely myself, when the nattering doubts and fears that have embedded themselves in my life are muted. It is only with her that I am at peace, and free.

Fifty-Three

I had never been in love with anyone until I met my wife. I came close with the rock star, but in all honesty, I wasn't capable of love until she shattered me to pieces, until every wall I had built around my heart was reduced to rubble, until I was on my knees and sobbing in the dust. And I will always love her for that. *Love*, I say, when I mean love, as though the heart only has one setting. As if there was a diction sufficient to contain this bursting. Love is a place where language fails.

To be fair, I don't think I was capable of shattering *her*. Whatever we intended when we started, we were always on different trajectories. I looked to her to shake myself from the fleeting, aimless evenings, the future's unresolved guitar chords. She looked to me as ... I don't know. A distraction, perhaps? A dalliance? I was younger than her, less established both in music and in life. Everything slipped through my fingers constantly. I was looking to stop that. I think she was looking to let go for a while.

The days leading up to the end felt like the tide receding before a wave crashes. I could feel something happening, but didn't put the pieces together right away. I had accompanied her band to a gig about an hour out of town, playing roadie. The first band was unmemorable, the sort of competent racket that's fine when you listen to it but is then forgotten before the next beer is poured. But between the bands was a poet, and that's where the trouble began.

He wasn't a particularly good writer, but he was that brand of mediocre that audiences respond to when it's delivered with enough bravado. The keyboardist for my girlfriend's band mooned over him his entire set. I disliked him instantly. The college English major in me lamented how writing that shallow and clichéd could be construed as poetry. The keyboardist told me she thought he was sexy. I thought he had a punchable face. The rock star, on the other hand, didn't seem to have much of an opinion about him at all. She was usually off inside her own head before performing.

She was spectacular, as always — a Joan Jett riot packed with sex and drugs and the wreckage they have always left behind. That was something she and I had in common — the human debris of friends lost to drugs and alcohol, the funerals and vanishings into rehab clinics. It was commonplace in the world where we lived, but she turned that dirge into something aching, angry and beautiful.

To my annoyance, we ended up at a Denny's with the other band and the poet, and I was forced to remain civil. I mostly didn't talk, allowing the keyboardist to flirt awkwardly, while the rock star talked music and set up a few more shows. The poet was connected to the music scene there, and happy to help. I tried not to roll my eyes.

The next few weeks devolved into our usual chaos with our bands playing opposing gigs, our schedules so convoluted that we didn't see each other for days, and definitely didn't catch each other's shows. We scraped out time, when we could, for frantic sex and Chinese takeaway, but the desperation of it all had me ill at ease. I wanted more, and couldn't even begin to figure out how to make that happen. So I did what I always did, and rode the tide to wherever it took me.

One night, one of the indie bands I sat in with opened for my girlfriend's band, and I was filling in on rhythm guitar. It was the first and only show we played on the same bill as a couple. We played our set, and then I went to help her band set up. They had played the night before with the poet and a couple other bands I didn't know, and I hadn't really heard how it went. As my rock star was busy getting herself together, I asked the keyboardist. She just shrugged. *It was OK,* she said, not sounding enthused. Trying to be polite, I asked after the poet. She just shook her head. *Yeah,* she said. *I tried, but he's hung up on someone else.* She then excused me to go get a beer before things started.

That band never put on a bad show. Not once. The crowd was enraptured, and a small mosh pit erupted at the foot of the stage. I watched from the back of the house, more impressed than ever. The club rang with applause as they finished their set. I walked to the side of the stage and kissed the rock star, as I always did. Her lips pressed hard against mine, more forcefully than usual. She wrapped her arms around me and held her body close against mine. I asked what was wrong, and she said *nothing*. When we got back to her place, we fucked in her garage, not even making it to the bedroom. She dug her nails into my arm and pulled me to her, and I bent her over the hood of her car. Then we gathered our tossed clothing and resumed in the bedroom. We watched the sun crack through her curtains in the morning. After breakfast at the deli she liked, I went back to my rented room.

I found myself in a state of peace that day, so mellow my roommate thought I was stoned. It wasn't something I'd been seeking, just a strange bliss that seemed to permeate my day. I found I wanted little, was content just to *be*. I was watching TV in the living room when the rock star called, apologizing that we wouldn't see each other than night. *It's cool*, I said. *I'm feeling remarkably Zen today. I don't think anything could bother me.* Her reply sounded dubious, but I told her I'd see her the next day, at a solo gig she had at the coffeehouse where I first saw her. I didn't say *I love you*. We *never* said that, although I was thinking it. And from this vantage, I'm glad. Not because I *didn't*, although as I've said, it was the closest I'd ever been to being in love, so close that I could be forgiven for thinking I was.

No, from the safety of this distance, I'm glad I didn't say it because it would have made what came next even harder for her, and even if I might not have thought it *then*, looking back I'm glad to have spared her that tiny sliver of pain.

Fifty-Four

There was no thunderclap moment when the guitars went away
for good, when they became ornaments of my home's private
spaces, reserved for quiet moments alone, or small gatherings
of friends. Their presence in my life simply dissolved over time,
although for some reason I can't bring myself to sell them or
give them away.

Freelance work gave way to a marketing job, banker's hours
and a steady paycheck. My life stopped accommodating music's
demands, and I wasn't cut out for a solo career, even a small one.
My voice isn't strong enough to carry a set, and I have no gift for
writing my own songs. The marketing job brought me
a house and food, a stability I had never known. It freed me from
the sickness in my stomach, the fear that this one real love I'd
found would slide from my grip and disappear. I love it for that,
although sometimes I think I love it in the way one loves any
cage, how after a while it's been there so long you can't imagine
life without it.

Sometimes, late at night, I imagine life without it, dream I've
found a chord progression that will shatter everything, let
me turn away from love and home and everything we've built
together. For a few moments, before I settle back to sleep,
I convince myself there is some freedom to be found on the other
side of demolition, some happiness I am missing even greater
than the one I already know. I think of our friend, who also
sometimes visits me at night, lips barely brushed against mine
until the shock of the touch awakens me, and wonder if I should
have reached for her that night, as we lay on the couch, pulled
her close and risked everything to kiss her. And then I wake,
and know the answer to that question.

I say love is the fact of a person, the way she permeates the architecture of your heart. Sometimes, in these moments when the fear settles in, and the urge to run threatens to overcome me, I will pull my wife close to me, kiss her forehead, and hold her until I drift away. Or sometimes I just let her sleep and count the thousand photographs that haunt the attic of my mind, retrace the thousand footsteps that led me here, this place of safety which is, for me, uncharted territory. Every day I wake and know this love is something more than I have ever known, and it's that knowledge that lets me keep the restlessness at bay, lets me walk forward into the undiscovered morning.

.

Fifty-Five

There was no passion when she kissed me. I said nothing —
she had a show to do — but I found the eerie calm in my head
giving way to a thousand spiders creeping on the edge of my
consciousness, and a sickness welling in my stomach, creeping
up my throat. I don't think I moved through her entire set,
don't recall a single note sung. All I recall from that long hour
waiting is how time slowed to a crawl, how all sound was muffled
and everything around me seemed to pop in vivid colors. I felt
seasick. I choked down the urge to vomit.

I don't think anyone around me could sense my distress. I'd
already become a ghost in the music, fading chorus refrained and
refrained at lower and lower volume, until the song doesn't so
much end as disappear entirely, as if it had never been there at
all. This was what was happening to *me*, and I think I knew it all
along.

And yet, there's a theater to this sort of breakup, a level where
you find yourself outside your body, watching as the pair of you
fall into the clichéd, predetermined script — *we need to talk* and
give me another chance and *I knew you were needy when we met.*
Then, the match-strike temper, the nasty insults I don't really
mean. There was a bile in my throat that I couldn't cough up,
a hurt so deep it needed to be released. She started crying, and
so did I, but her tears dabbed her eyes and mine soaked my face.
And then, the ultimate cliché, so bad I can't believe I'd brought
myself to say it: *How could you?*

How could she what? the weird, rational part of my brain watching
the scene from the outside asked. Bow to the inevitable end of
a relationship that you and she both knew was doomed from
the start? Acknowledge that we'd been straying in different
directions for weeks? *Hurt me?* And there it was, the shape of
the thing I couldn't perceive — how every stab of loneliness and
longing, every sorrow and sadness I'd ever felt, each of them
echoed in that wound.

I was a teenager again, and the first girl I'd ever been intimate with at all has walked away from me, and I'm in college again, and the woman I'd been hung up on for ages is fucking another guy in her dorm room, and I am every heartbreak I have ever been, all of them, a chorus of voices muffled under my skin — *I'm sorry* and *forgive me* and *I love you, I love you, I love you.* These were words I never said to anyone, because I didn't think I believed them. But in that moment, I believed them. Also – *I forgive you.* I was sometimes the villain in the story, true, but not always. I am owed an apology for every apology I owe. I can think of no parting where we didn't scald each other, where neither of us walked away burned. *I love you, I forgive you, I'm sorry, forgive me.* All the times I never said those things now broke the surface of my skin, overwhelming me, driving me to my knees.

And yet, we were also what we appeared to be: Two people in a parking lot, lovers parting ways. I gibbered with pain, incoherent mess that had pretended for years to be a man, and she was overcome with grief, horror struck at just how shattered I was, and yet, beneath it all, regretted nothing.

In hours or in minutes, some unit of time beyond my comprehension, I regained my composure, enough pain having bled from my skin. I stood and dusted myself off, as though I'd simply tripped. She granted me the dignity of saying nothing. I asked if there was someone else, and she told me of the poet, how they'd been circling each other since they met, but that nothing had happened. She wanted to break things off with me, first.

I nodded, and lit a cigarette, pondering the weight of *nothing*, how the negative space of it became a wall between us. The nicotine cleared my head, and although my face was still soaked, the tears stopped. *OK*, I said, and she didn't ask *OK, what?* I got it. I understood. But all I could say was *OK*. The flattest, most noncommittal acknowledgment I could possibly muster, but it was literally all I was capable of saying.

Are you going to be OK? she asked, and I shook my head. *No,* I said, then shrugged. *Yeah. Eventually.* There were pieces of me littering the parking lot, tiny bits of people I've been, blowing away in the wind. I took a drag and turned away from her to look in the windows of the coffeehouse. I could see her playing on the stage, her back toward me, body a taunt wire, electrified. And I could see myself in the audience, captivated.

I locked eyes with myself, through the glass and across the months, and both of us understood that I was no longer that person, that he had become a distant memory already, that love and loss has transformed us completely. Another drag, and he was gone. I turned again to face the rock star, and began to laugh, a maniacal cackle that came from nowhere. And then she laughed, too, and we hollered like lunatics. She opened her arms to hug me, and I surrendered. I surrendered everything.

She opened her car door and said goodbye. I told her the poet's writing sucks. She laughed, but didn't deny it. She drove away, and I mouthed the words I should have said: *I'm sorry, I forgive you, I love you, forgive me.*

Fifty-Six

At 40, the doorman doesn't even ask me for an ID. No one blinks when I order a beer. I look around the club, and everywhere there are young people with X's marked on the back of their hands. Nothing's really changed, except me. Me and the music, and how we relate. My young musician friend, who's band my wife and I are here to see, tells me it's all just rock 'n' roll to him, but I tell him there are differences now — what were major keys have become minor, going soft where the traditional rock impulse would be to go loud. I point out that he himself borrows chord structures from Eastern Europe folk music now, rather than ripping them straight from blues. That happened much more rarely 20 years ago.

I tell him rock has gotten old, and that musicians now look in different places to keep things fresh. It happens. Anything that stays the same for too long stagnates and dies. He asks me why I don't play guitar anymore, and I just shrug. *I chose to change,* I say. And he laughs, as if it were a punch line. Maybe it is. After all, almost everything I am today, the entirety of this strange, quiet, mostly happy life, started with a joke. That's never been lost on me. And yet, as he climbs on stage and straps on his guitar, soundchecks himself against the cacophony of horns and percussion, the unruly mob of music he's surrounded himself with, I find it hard not to feel a twinge of jealousy, the low hum pulse of nostalgia. I find my fingers ghosting the chords to *Layla,* or *Satisfaction,* or *(What's So Funny 'Bout) Peace, Love, and Understanding.* Songs I only vaguely remember how to play. I'm not that guy anymore, but he whispers to me sometimes, his major keys a counterpoint to my minors. His voice goes loud when mine goes quiet.

That's the truth about rock 'n' roll: The volume and the aggression will always return. It will always revert to pianos banging at a breakneck pace in a brothel. For every Led Zeppelin there is an equal and opposite Ramones, a Johnny Thunders for every Clapton. Rock 'n' roll is and always has been a great leveler. Its primary purpose is to burn things down. It wasn't so long ago that it reduced the awkward child I was to ash.

My young musician friend is a bit of a pied piper — his band seems like a gaggle of children to me, but they're probably all older than I was when I was first dragged into a club like this. Absently, I wonder if they're even old enough to be in here, but then I realize I probably wasn't old enough to be in half the places I was when I was young. *They* probably have permission, because they're performing. Back when I was young, no one checked if you weren't being stupid.

The music starts in earnest, and my wife's artist friend drags her by the hand to join the rush of bodies heading to the front of the stage to dance. I stay behind and nurse my beer. The music is upbeat and jaunty, and it moves at a breakneck pace. The young crowd writhes and twirls to the beat, and it strikes me that, if nothing else, it's more aesthetic to watch than slam dancing ever was. Sometimes I miss the aggression of it all, but when I stumble into a hardcore show, I often find that nostalgia better left in the past.

The artist is only slightly younger than my wife and me, but you'd never know it to look at her. There's a youthfulness about her that never seems to dim, an air of taking joy in almost everything she does, even when she's miserable. And I have to remind myself she's miserable now, dancing out some boy or other who broke her heart. I never met this one. Sometimes, I can't keep track of the men and women in her life, although she always seems sincerely in love with them. The ease with which she loves is startling, sometimes. She makes friends easily, often instantly. People are drawn to her openness, her bright smile and sharp intelligence. But I think, sometimes, the men and women she dates don't see the entirety of her at first, how they're never really going to measure up to her first love, which is painting. Whether they end it or she does, they only ever seem to be there until they're in the way of the next work of art, until that muse calls her and art once again consumes her attention.

Part of me is a little jealous of that, too, as jealous as I am of the guitar on stage blasting through folk songs to arrangements scored for methamphetamine. She lets nothing distract her from her artwork, when I gave *everything* else priority. In her honest, drunken moments, she confesses she regrets some of her decisions, but not really. She knows she'd do the same thing twice. *In a different color scheme*, she adds, smiling mischievously. *Maybe next time in mauve.*

She and my wife dance with abandon. I can never keep up with her on the dance floor, and sometimes I fear that disappoints, that we don't dance as often as we could, that she doesn't often dance as well as she *can*. Perhaps everyone sacrifices pieces of their selves for love, the odds and ends that don't fit well in marriage's new house. But those things we've abandoned never really disappear entirely. They linger like the last note of a song, hanging in the air impossibly long.

My wife lost touch with most of her friends from her painting days. Her life changed when she stopped making art, and everyone's lives moved on in different directions. The artist was different, though. She refused to shuffle out of my wife's life when their interests diverged. *I'm not as shallow as I look*, she said of it one night, when my wife raised the question. *I'm already living my life. I don't need my friends to live it, too.*

I could always see why my wife loved her a little, even forgetting that there was always a smoldering between them that never quite extinguished. Sometimes, I figure I should be jealous of that heat, but I can never quite work up to it. It seems to be something they live with easily, a piece of who they were that lingered, never quite finding the right shelf on which to be stored. And sometimes, when I look at their bond, at the obvious attraction they reflexively keep at bay, I wonder how much of herself my wife has sacrificed to be in love with *me*, how deep those cracks run beyond my mere reluctance to dance.

I can be a lot of things, but I can never be *her*. That part of my wife's life is a mystery to me, one I have no idea how to unravel, or if I even should.

Fifty-Seven

Every day as mundane and miraculous as breathing — common, invisible thing that keeps me alive. Alarm clock. Alarm clock. Alarm clock. Creak of body, slow-motion animation. Hungry cat mewling. Pour kibble, pour water, scoop litter box, wash hands. Prescriptions, multiplying as I pass 40. Tuesdays, trash.

Last night's dishes. Kettle. Filtered water. Pot of tea — green, caffeine–free; French press coffee, one cup. Whistle of boiling water. Kiss wife awake. Bowl of granola cereal, banana maybe, sometimes orange. Weekends, bacon and eggs. Scrambled, or sunny side up. Not omelets. Never come out right. Doesn't matter. She doesn't much care for eggs.

Separate offices. Newspaper online. Favorite blogs. Email. Interrupt each other to share funny videos. Brush teeth. Floss. Shower. Button-down shirt, solid colors. Jeans. Kiss goodbye. Say *I love you.* Mean it, even when it seems a muscle twitch, automatic response, just a handful of words. Drive. Traffic. Stop. Surreptitious doughnut. More coffee, this time with cream. Drive. Traffic. Parking pass. Stop. Smoke.

Computer. Marketing. Pointless emails. Dull conversation. Feigned interest in baseball. Fantasize about sex. Comprehend workplace affairs: Anything to feel alive. Anything to not feel *here.* Drudgery. Small triumph. Pointless emails. Irrelevant meeting. Elvis Costello song, stuck in my head. Call home. Ascertain it's a normal day. Check shopping list on smartphone. Leave. Smoke. Traffic. Store. Onions. Olive oil. Wine.

Park. Climb stairs. Open door. Make joke less witty than imagined. Kiss wife. Hold her. Say *I love you.* Mean it. Wonder, briefly, what we are in separate rooms, what underscores the fact of us. Ask about her day. Share mine in bullet points.

Lose myself in the hubbub of chores. Odd days, make dinner. Protein. Starch. Vegetable. She cooks better. Maybe take-out, if one of us works late. Chinese, sometimes Indian. Drawer full of menus.

Shuffle songs on iPod. Random music, mostly old. Played guitar once. Barely remember it. Imagine being that person. Thought slips away. Flip pork chops at three-minute intervals. Leave potatoes in boiling water for 15 minutes. Strain. Mash. Frozen peas, with a little butter. Salt.

Eat in front of television. Last night's *Daily Show*, handful of sitcoms, maybe a drama. Recline on the couch. She curls against me. Head rests on shoulder. Kiss her. She laughs. Kiss her again. TV. Fast-forward through commercials. Clean up dinner. Leave dishes for morning. Brush teeth. Floss. Slide into bed. Read. She comes to bed, after video games. Reads. We kiss goodnight. Sometimes sex. Sometimes sleep. Say *I love you* before nighttime takes me. Mean it, real as water or bone, as sunlight or skin. Say it easily as breathing. Sleep until morning. Alarm clock. Alarm clock. Alarm clock.

This peace is uncharted territory. Common as salt, but something I had ever known before. I find it miraculous. Each day I wake with my lips kissed by ocean.

Fifty-Eight

The music ends and I order another beer before the crowd gravitates back to the bar, grabbing my wife a gin and tonic while I'm at it. I hand it to her when she and the artist return, sweating and joyous from dancing. I'm greeted with a delighted smile and a peck on the lips. She takes a sip and sees friends across the room. She says *love you* as she excuses herself, and I repeat the words back, settling into a chair at a table. the artist, who has obtained a glass of whiskey seemingly without ordering, slides into the chair across from me.

I love you guys, she says, sipping her drink. An uninformed observer might think she's tipsy, but I know better. She can pound liquor down when she wants to. Right now, she's just letting herself be bubbly. *You make me actually believe in marriage.*

Hey, now, I say, snickering lightly. *That's not any pressure to put on someone, is it?* I'm kind of joking, kind of not. *We never claimed to be any sort of role models.*

She has this sort of mock-innocent expression she uses when she's called on anything she says. Her eyes get wide and her mouth opens in shock that *anything* she said could be so misconstrued. She crooks her head one way, then another, elongating her neck, shrugging her shoulders a little. I have to admit, it's stupidly attractive. Part of me wishes she weren't so likable, this woman who could have been my wife's lover had just a few cards come up different. Part of me wishes I were prone to jealousy.

I'm just saying you guys are great, she says, offering a smile that's equal parts girlish and flirty. She's having fun tonight, blowing off steam. I've long learned not to make anything of her flirtatiousness, even if I can't help but find myself a *little* taken. I've always seen what my wife sees in her, and why they've worked to remain friends. It's odd, pulling someone else's lust off the shelf to contemplate, this keepsake they can't quite bear to throw away. I have a few of those myself, I suppose — photos in a box in the attic, gathering dust. But *this* is different. This woman is real, wearing a flowing gypsy dress straight out of Stevie Nicks' closet, dirty-blonde hair done up in a bun. She is not a hypothetical situation. She's sitting across from me, drinking whiskey. I thank her for the compliment, and change the subject, asking how she's doing.

She takes a swig and recounts the latest of her doomed relationships, and it's hard for me to not be struck by how sincere her heartbreak always is, even though everyone else can usually see the expiration date stamped on the guy or girl's forehead. She never sees it like that, and I suppose the fact that she sees things different than everybody else is one of the things that makes her such a great artist. But no, she loves people fully and unreservedly. Her love is a tornado. She and everyone around her get swept up in it. And afterward, there's usually ruin.

She recounts the story, but I'm only half-listening, my attention drawn to a girl in the crowd — flash of dyed-black hair and white makeup. The taste of gin and lemons appears on my lips as the girl crosses my line of vision — walking memory, the first girl I ever kissed, looking exactly as she did when we first met, 25 years ago. It's impossible, of course. She'd be my age now, not this skinny teenager still. Was she really that frail? She seemed ghostlike then, but that was a long time ago, and I was still overwhelmed by the phantasmagoria of it all, dark theater of shadows on the wall.

The girl vanishes, and I wonder if I just imagined her. The artist is still talking, and I am nodding sympathetically, even mouthing words of encouragement and validation. I try to put the girl out of my head, but it doesn't work.

It's not the first time I've seen her. Every now and again, I catch a glimpse of her out of the corner of my eye, odd phantom of my youth whose name I never knew. I've been searching for her ever since she disappeared. I'm not entirely sure what I would do if I found her — it's doubtful she remembers me at all, and anyway, she's probably not the person she was. People change in 25 years. She could be anything — a soccer mom, a lawyer, a waitress, a nuclear physicist, a junkie, a chef. She could be happy somewhere, or miserable, or a cog in a machine that spins and whirls with clockwork precision.

But wherever she is, and whatever her life, one thing is certain: She is *not* waiting for me. She doesn't know me any more than I know her, even though she changed the course of my entire life. How would you begin to explain that to a stranger? How do you tell someone that you think of them every time a power chord is strummed, each time percussion falls like a jackhammer?

The artist rises from her seat, and says she's off to fetch another drink. She leans over and kisses me chastely on the cheek. *Thanks for listening*, she says, then drifts toward the bar, leaving me distracted and small, unsure what's stirring beneath my skin.

Fifty-Nine

Her kiss is bourbon with a hint of mint, unexpected outcrop of spring in winter, glint of sunlight in the snow. It comes sudden, and unexpected. I am shocked that I return it with force, body a coiled spring. One arm wraps around her waist, pulling her close, the other rests on the back of her head, fingers running through her hair.

If there is a context for this, I have forgotten it. Can't even remember where I am or how we came to be here. It's just me, and the artist, and a bottomless pit we keep trying to fill. She smiles, and there's a nervousness I've never seen on her face before. Her hands fiddle with my shirt's buttons. I kiss her again, slide a hand underneath her blouse.

There is a version of me standing off to the side of this, observing, wondering about the guilt I should be feeling, amazed at how, in these moments, everything else vanishes. We could be in a hotel room, or a broom closet, or the bathroom of a seedy nightclub, and it wouldn't matter. There is a buzz in our brains that drowns out everything, skin in a state of electroshock. My lips descend to her neck while one hand works its way beneath her dress. She shivers, throws back her head as if to scream, but instead bites her bottom lip. She makes a squeak, and her hand rubs against my jeans' zipper, fumbling to undo my belt. We are a tangle of clothes and exposed skin. For a moment, we disappear entirely.

We end in a flurry of kisses, each one lighter than the last, until our lips are simply kissing air. We hold each other, but say nothing. She dresses and leaves. I remain, naked amid discarded clothing.

I light a cigarette, and turn to face my wife. Her countenance is blank. I search her eyes for a spark of anger, or betrayal, or *anything*, but find nothing. From outside my body, I watch myself mouth my weak confession, the words moths, taking to flight. She says nothing. She doesn't scream, doesn't cry, just stares at me with an expression I can't discern. I have no idea what is going on inside her head. I have no idea if I should stay or gather up my clothes and leave.

My stomach churns. I quickly turn away from my wife and vomit. The force with which it comes is alarming. My whole body spasms, until I am on my knees dry heaving, drained and shivering.

I look up toward my wife, but realize that she has gone, and all I can hear are bells tolling in the distance, a wedding or a funeral, one or the other, drowning out the din of my all-too-present mind.

Alarm clock. Alarm clock. Alarm clock.

Eyes snap open.

Fuck.

Sixty

A marriage changes nothing. You are still the same person you were before the ceremony, before the first kiss, before you even met each other. It is only the wanting to change that makes it so.

But sometimes even *wanting* to change isn't enough. My desire to change was a wildfire, reducing my history to ash. But in some ways, that's just another arson. I can feel the chaos and loneliness burning underneath my skin, calling to be released. There is a part of me that always wants to be alone again amid the cinders.

Sixty-One

My wife and I join the artist for sushi, then back to her place for
bourbon. She has *excellent* taste in whiskey, so it's an easy sell.
Within a few minutes, the muscles in our backs and shoulders
loosen, and we sprawl on her couches amid half-painted canvases,
listening to music and talking about art. She shows us the latest
work in progress, a thin, proud smile on her face as my wife
gushes. I like it, but I don't know much about art. She puts on
a Nina Simone album — vinyl, naturally — and refreshes our
drinks.

I try not to make a show of watching her hips move as she passes,
concentrating instead on the glass in my hand, I've already
shoved my dream of her down into some dark place where it
can't do any damage, but even still, a piece of me shudders when
I see her, even if that shuddering is stupid and useless. She
and my wife continue talking about painting, about color and
composition, in terms that I only barely understand. Then, they
talk about her love life, how she's been single for weeks, which
may well be some sort of record.

I'm painting, she says, nonchalantly. *That makes being single easy. I
f I weren't painting right now, I'm sure it would be different.*

She brings fresh bourbon, and flounces onto the couch facing us.

I've got a question, she asks, a devil in her smile. *Have you guys ever
dated a woman? Like, as a couple?*

She giggles as she says it, that odd mix of sophistication and
playfulness lacing her voice. My wife and I both stop and start
to respond, exaggerating our wordlessness with comically
exaggerated shock, as if the question were a joke. But it isn't.
Not really. And its implications aren't lost on anyone in the room.

I tell myself it's the whiskey talking, but the same bottle of bourbon is loosening my tongue, too, so I answer honestly: *No*. She and my wife have been circling each other since before I met them, an *almost* hanging over them each time they hug, each time one of them touches the other's hand. And even though my wife says she's moved past that attraction, part of me can't help but wonder ...

I intellectualize, explain how I don't believe it would be right to put someone in the middle of our marriage, how any other relationship would, by definition, have to come second. *I can't see why anyone would want that*, I say. My wife just shrugs and says, *Besides. Women are hard.*

The artist laughs, and nods in understanding, and begins to hypothesize ways it could work. Abstractly. I agree in theory, but tell her people are complicated, and that reason has never held an adequate tether on the heart. She agrees, and goes to fetch another bottle of whiskey. I take the opportunity to step out for a cigarette. My wife joins me, although she hasn't smoked in over a year, blaming the whiskey as she rises.

Is she hitting on both of us? she asks as soon as we're outside, and saying it out loud makes the whole situation more surreal. And silently, I consider how much she's gotten under my skin lately, and for a second, the other night's dream emerges from the pit where it was banished, and I can feel my heartbeat quicken.

I can taste the want in the air. It lingers like my cigarette smoke, nearly visible in the moonlight. My wife and I both agree that if it would work with *anyone*, it would be *her*.

We have the length of a cigarette burning to confer. I list my priorities — not damaging our marriage, not hurting anyone, including both of them. Including myself. Somehow, the ticking clock of it all makes the conversation easier, more businesslike. There is no time for awkwardness. My wife asks if I'm interested, and I admit I am. She thinks about it, and confesses she isn't. And that pretty much ends things. *I just don't think I could handle it*, she says, and I nod. I get it. *I actually think it would be easier if you and she just had a thing*. I kiss her, but don't answer. There's a charge in the air that's familiar and frightening. It's the feeling you get when something is about to break.

Sixty-Two

When the rock star shattered me in a coffeehouse parking lot,
I became a stone-faced somnambulist, the shambling dead,
a landslide. I crumbled at the lightest touch, suffered erosion
when kissed by air. I was exposed, unshielded from the wind,
storm-tossed and broken.

And I was being beaten at checkers by a 10-year-old girl.

The girl's mother was a barista at the same coffeehouse where
I became a ghost, and I had taken to haunting the place. I
couldn't tell you why. Maybe I was hoping to see the rock star
again, although it wasn't somewhere she frequented if she didn't
have a gig. She had other haunts, and I stayed clear of them, even
bars I had discovered first. Maybe I was caught in some sort
of loop, trying to angle myself backward in time, searching for
some way to negate history, to wake up one morning and find
some way for the pain to have never happened.

I asked the art student out to a movie, unsure if I even wanted
anything. She called me on my bullshit with undeserved
kindness, disappearing and taking a chapter of my history with
her. I contemplated seeking out other old lovers, but couldn't
dredge up the strength. I didn't even really want the rock star
anymore. There was an emptiness in my chest where I kept her
memory, recalled the smoothness of her skin, the smell of her
hair. I could remember her kiss and how her cunt tasted. I could
resurrect these memories in minute detail, but they no longer
meant anything. Just old movies I saw late at night, on television,
when I couldn't sleep.

The 10-year-old was usually bored, waiting for her mother to finish work, and few of the regulars were reluctant to entertain her with a board game if they weren't otherwise occupied. I was never otherwise occupied, and hadn't played checkers in years. She slaughtered me, every game, to her continued delight. I had started out taking it easy, but after a while, I was playing to win. Not that it helped.

Nothing helped, not even music. I played now with preternatural precision, hitting each note flawlessly, keeping perfectly in time. Keeping time is easy when it's standing still. I could see the notes suspended in space in front of me. They should have been beautiful, but right then, they were merely mathematics.

Friends dragged me out after gigs, and I floated along for the ride – poor company, but present. I could sit in a crowded Denny's booth at 2 a.m. like a pro. You don't really need to do much if everyone else is talking. And everybody was *always* talking.

I wondered, sometimes, if the 10-year-old was lonely. It seems an odd life, hanging around her mother's work most days after school, with no one her own age to talk to. I knew a few things – knew her parents were divorced and that her father was … somewhere. Out of the picture. Neither of them ever spoke of him. I knew her mother played bass – I even played a gig with a band she was in, once – but she didn't play much anymore. *Too many more important things to do*, she said, when I asked her if she missed it. I said that wasn't an answer, and she just smiled, shook her auburn bangs out of her face and adjusted her glasses.

One night, after a show, this guy who always hung out with the punk band pulled me aside and asked if I was doing anything that night. I shook my head, and he nodded in the direction of two goth girls. He'd been talking to one of them all night, and she was game to go somewhere, but she wasn't willing to abandon her friend. My head snowed with all the reasons this was a bad idea, and I couldn't muster enthusiasm for a single one of them, so I said *sure.*

The guy wasn't really a *friend*. We'd never really hung out before. He was a messed up punk with some bad habits, and he'd always kind of gotten on my nerves. But he was desperately in need of a wing man. *Just a few drinks*, he said. *Maybe hang out a bit. I'll drive.*

I floated along, and I honestly couldn't tell you why. The girls seemed nice enough, the one the annoying punk was hitting on was bubbly and sarcastic, which was actually an amusing combination. Her friend was quiet – not really *shy*, but mostly she just listened as her friend did most of the talking. Which suited me fine. Their goth drag was thrift store cheap, and their makeup was smudged. They had a ragged edge about them that was actually interesting.

Very little *interested* me at that time. I found the barista interesting, wondered how anyone could give up music, how she found the strength to do so much on her own. She was slightly older than me, and had a geekiness about her, her sleight build and wire-frame glasses giving her a bookish air. She even had it when she played, I recalled, a sort of rock 'n' roll librarian vibe. It was striking. You don't forget that easily.

The goth girl my acquaintance was pursuing had a studio apartment on the outskirts of town, and the four of us crowded into the tiny space with a bottle of wine. She had a sleeper sofa, which was pulled out when we arrived. She didn't offer to fold it back into a couch as she and the punk sat on the edge of the bed and her friend and I sat on the floor, amid strewn dirty laundry and linens, pillows tossed indiscriminately on the floor.

Sisters of Mercy crooned from her stereo: *Pain looks great on other people/ that's what they're for.* We poured more wine into plastic cups, and within a few minutes, the pair of them were making out on the bed. The two of us sat quietly, unsure exactly what we should to do.

It was late. I wasn't wasted, but it was too far to walk home at night, and I didn't have enough money for a cab. The goth beside me shot me a look as the pair of them pawed each other, then shrugged her shoulders. I laughed a little, and we gathered some of the strewn pillows and blankets as the pair above us moaned and grunted.

The girl beside me giggled, and I couldn't help but smile. It was ridiculous. She rolled closer and kissed me, and I kissed her back, and soon we were grinding our clothed bodies against one another, wordless, lost in the moment.

She wasn't the first woman I'd kissed since the rock star left me. Once, when I helped the barista take the trash out back, she leaned in close and pressed her lips against mine. It was an impulse, and it startled us both. We kissed again, and then stopped, then returned to the coffeehouse as though nothing had happened.

The goth girl and I stayed silent as the other pair made a racket. I slipped my hand underneath her blouse and rubbed her small breasts. She bit my shoulder, and I rolled on top of her, dry-humping her to the chorus of other people having sex. I couldn't really see the other couple, but it was clear that they were naked while we were mostly clothed. If it had just been us, we would have prob ably been naked already. But disrobing in front of *three* people was … awkward.

I didn't know where this was leading, and in all honesty, I didn't really care. The barista and I had developed a thing where we made out for a few minutes behind the coffeehouse, and then returned, but we never *went* anywhere. We weren't an item. I was single, and there was a lithe young woman underneath me, and I wanted someone else to make decisions for me.

If the goth had wanted me to stop, I would have. If she had wanted me to rip her clothes off and fuck her properly, I would have. If she had wanted us to climb into bed with the others, I would have. I'd have quite willingly become driftwood between their bodies, would have fucked all three of them, or none of them, and it wouldn't have made a bit of difference. I didn't much care what happened, and that was kind of frightening. How can you surrender to *want* and still feel nothing? Is it really *want* at all? This is a place where language fails.

The goth girl beneath me bit her lower lip as my pelvis rubbed against hers, arching her back in time to my thrusting. I came in my jeans, then reached my hand down her skirt to finish her off. Both of us choked down the sound of our orgasms, holding each other close in silence as the marathon above us raged on, somehow drifting off to sleep.

I didn't see either of the girls again, and never really talked much to my acquaintance afterward, either. But when I arrived at the coffeehouse the next day, it was hard to pretend nothing had happened. My checkers nemesis and I began our customary game, but I was even more distracted than usual. And she noticed. *Are you OK?* she asked, and I told her I just had a lot on my mind. *Ah,* she said, knowingly, in that way that kids always seem to have your number. I lost some more checkers, and then, out of the blue, she asked, *Are you and my mom dating?*

The girl came sharply into focus as my breathing shallowed. She was a pint-sized version of her mother, with the same sharpness. I didn't want to lie to her, but the previous night was replaying in my head, and I felt seasick. *It's OK if you are,* she said;. *You're a lot nicer than the other guys she's dated,* and I had absolutely no idea how to respond.

I don't know, I said as honestly as I could. *I don't think so. I think we're really just friends.*

Ah, she said, as though this were no big surprise. *That's cool.*
And then she continued playing, wiping the floor with me. When
I helped her mother with the trash that night, she came in for a
kiss, but I stopped her. I asked her if this was going somewhere –
if she even *wanted* it to go somewhere. She thought about it, and
asked if I was asking her out on a real date. It hadn't occurred to
me, but I supposed I was. She thought about it, and then shook
her head.

I'm sorry, she said. *This is all I can handle right now.*

And I nodded. I understood completely. *I think I need more than
this,* I said, not quite believing the words. *I think it's time for me to
start living life again.*

She nodded, then hugged me, and I held her for a moment, before
letting her go.

It was fun, though, she said. *Wasn't it?*

It was. And I didn't really want to leave, but I could hear clocks
ticking again, could feel time wake from its slumber, trudging
into the future. It was time to move.

Sixty-Three

The last drags of the cigarette burn to ash, and we go back inside, where my wife's friend has changed the music to old Motown, much to my delight. We chatter about Diana Ross, about The Four Tops, Stevie Wonder and The Spinners, Marvin Gaye and the Jackson Five, about that great, soulful music that permeates our culture, that's become so ubiquitous we often forget how amazing it was, how it distilled love and sex down into something pure and beautiful, music so vivid it reached across all barriers, burrowed into the heart of anyone who really listened. I confess that, for me, this is the music that burns at the center of rock 'n' roll, that burst of passion and honesty that flares in the dark, a burning humanity that transcends race and class. That transcends everything. Martha and the Vandellas come on the stereo, singing one of my favorites: *Calling out around the world ... are you ready for a brand new beat ... summer's here ... and the time is right ... for dancing in the streets ...*

It is 2 a.m., and we are more than tipsy, singing along with Martha Reeves. I say that *this* is the music that pulses in rock's bloodstream, that surges beneath each ornate classic rock guitar solo, each baroque prog.-rock instrumental or punk rock explosion of anger. This is rock's heartbeat, the spark of life that invigorates it all. We can dress it up a thousand ways, a thousand upon a thousand, but this is everything we're ever trying to say: *All we need is music ... sweet music ... and there's music everywhere ...*

I throw my head back and laugh, a rich, honest laugh that comes from the bottom of my stomach. And they're laughing, too — the three of us suspended in a moment of joy.

The song ends, and we drift back to our previous discussion, and I find myself telling the story of myself and our friend, alone on the couch, how there was a moment there that was meaningful beyond mere lust, a spark that had a tangible meaning, and how I let the moment go. The artist flicks her eyes to my wife, then asks if I regret that. I say *no*, then *yes*, then shake my head, unsure. *I think I regret not telling her*, I say. *That there was no way to have that conversation.* And my wife nods, and tells the story of her rock star, about how she reached for him and singed her fingertips.

We're so fragile, sometimes, she says, her voice trailing, as if she were lost in thought. *We break much easier than we think we do.*

Her friend nods, and I confess this silence is a sort of lying, but I don't know any other way to navigate these waters. I'm not really willing to pay the consequences of heartbreak, of the damage that sort of honesty incurs. I don't explicitly state that I'm lying now, that I can sense her want, and that part of me reciprocates, but she nods in understanding anyway, glances at the clock and says, *I should get to bed.* We're too trashed to drive, so we sleep on her sofa bed in the living room. We hug our friend goodnight, and it's a warm, loving embrace, one with no pretext or agenda.

Deep in the night, when all around is silence, my wife's hand reaches toward my crotch, begins to fumble with my zipper. I reach for her before my eyes snap open, but neither of us make a sound, not wanting to wake our host. Quietly, nervously, we become teenagers again, groping each other in the dark.

Sixty-Four

Permission burns in my throat as my wife kisses me on the
cheek and heads out to run errands with the artist, to keep her
company while she buys new brushes and acrylics, new canvases
and lacquer. I suggest she buy some new paints herself, but she
shrugs and kisses me goodbye. She's meeting the artist at her
place, and part of me bristles at the lost opportunity to see her.

When I met my wife, she had been dating a ninja, and I'd just
finished dating a magician's assistant. Both had a talent for
shadows and silence. Both were prone to disappearing.

 I am not so good at letting anything vanish. Everything
stays with me forever, it seems, a tide in my chest, ebbing and
flowing in severity, but never entirely gone. Sometimes my skin
remembers a touch I haven't felt in years, or I suddenly recall the
smell of someone's hair, ineffable aroma of oranges and mangoes.
Sometimes, at night, when I lie awake listening to my wife
breathe, I see all their faces cascade in the darkness, one by one,
every botched romance and might-have-been, every mistake and
small series of incisions. I see the artist's face among them,
and am seasick with want.

My wife and I weren't waiting patiently for one another.
She was circling a hipster guy who was studying to be a teacher,
or a social worker, or something. He was nice, but she didn't
have strong feelings for him. I was surrendering to a beautiful
businesswoman who – through no fault of her own – made me
too aware of the poverty inside myself, the way I could see my
failures reflected in her eyes. I could see how disposable I was.

My wife's lover was too tepid, mine cut my fingers when I
touched her. We found each other in a crowd, and one dumb joke
irrevocably changed our lives, washed away everything that came
before that moment.

I have tried to ask her if the past haunts her the same way
it haunts me, but the question never forms correctly, and we
instead devolve to war stories, comical tails of lust-driven follies.
In silence, I can believe we are the same sort of haunted – I know
her rock star, after all, know she still picks over unanswered
questions. But when I try to give the words life, they become
misplaced, like that novel you left somewhere in the living room,
that pair of glasses you swore was on the kitchen table.

Marriage didn't change who we were. Not really. And I know in
my heart I'm a dog that's been heeling for years, that *want* still
quivers underneath my skin.

I see the artist on my periphery everywhere: At the office,
lingering by the empty desk, the one I pretend isn't there. I see
her in the nightclubs, flash of skirt disappearing in the crowd.
I hear her on the radio, in all the pop star melodrama, think of
her as I kiss my wife and settle to sleep, touch my wife's hair and
remember the abyss, what I was before we met. The wreckage is
always close to the surface. Part of me is always homesick for it.

My wife, three-quarters asleep, turns and kisses my cheek, then
drifts off to slumber again. For a moment, my head is quiet,
and I can finally fall asleep.

Sixty-Five

Love listens, and this is how you love a woman who is not your wife: Distracted by background noise, garbled in static, power ballad at the bottom of the radio dial. You love in grace notes, filling space you never knew existed.

And this is how you love your wife when you also love another woman: Favorite song turned unfamiliar, shifting time signatures, melody transposed from piano to guitar. She is signal – she is *always* signal – but there are parts you must relearn.

These loves aspire to harmony in counterpoint. Played true, nothing clashes. Only dishonesty brings dissonance, but alas, that comes easily. You fall out of key. Your hands fumble, and you lose the beat. You repeat a verse. Turn, and you're a record skipping.

Your hands reach for chords you barely remember. Sometimes they connect softly, with a shudder, with whispered prayers. And sometimes they hit sloppily and flat, taking you out of the song entirely. And worse: You hit every note correctly, then look to see your fingers bleeding.

You listen to your heart, as they say, but its percussion pounds too fast, and echoes across an empty chamber. Your heart is an idiot, and can't help you. It simply wants to thrash until it falls, exhausted.

It is *all* exhausting. You fiddle with balance: More bass, more treble, and for a moment you have it perfect and it's beautiful and clear. For a moment you are breathless, and at peace. But it passes too soon. The song unravels. You try to gather up the strands, but they've dissolved.

You start again. You try to love a woman who is not your wife, and you try to love your wife when you're in love with another woman, and you force yourself to wonder if you're actually listening to either and not just your own blood. You hear the ghost of a symphony, but composing it is beyond you. You end up standing still in silence.

Sixty-Six

We suffer because nothing happened. And we suffer because *nothing* happened. That is the totality of the thing.

Sixty-Seven

It started with a joke. It started with a whiskey-drenched
question that lingered too long. It started with a hurricane-
soaked wedding, and a break in the sky. It started with a Goth
girl in a noisy nightclub whom I would never see again. It
started with the casual sex of young strangers in a rented room.

It started when I put down the guitar. It started with the ache of
not pursuing a woman in arm's reach. It started with not lying.
It started in the absence of fear, in inexplicable trust, in an honest
weeping I never believed possible.

This love is a cascade of beginnings, each one igniting the rest.
I love, and every love I've felt before, no matter how sleight, boils
to the surface, rises from the depths like some Stygian monster.
And every silence pings at me, the roiling hurricane
of everything I've ever left unsaid, every silence embedded in my
skin. Every *I'm sorry*, each *I forgive you*, every *forgive me* and
I love you, all of them cluster on my tongue, longing to be spoken,
to express the thunderstorm of every heartbreak, every time
I broke a heart. To beg forgiveness of every trespass I've ever
made, and to forgive each trespass against me. To give a voice
to this thunderous gratitude for every love I've ever felt, no
matter how seemingly insignificant. All of them have made me
what I am. Each of them is an inflection in this love I feel now,
this thing that is greater than myself, all notes in the only song
I've written, the one we all write — aria of what is good in us,
echoing out against the horizon.

Sixty-Eight

I stand on the back porch, smoke a cigarette and stare between trees at the highway in the distance, anonymous cars driving to unknowable locations. Through the kitchen window behind me, *Save It for Later* by The English Beat is playing, a song from my youth, a song I loved beyond all reason before I was old enough to divine its meaning.

Two-dozen other stupid reasons
why we should suffer for this ...
don't bother trying to explain them ...
just hold my hand while I come
to a decision on it ...

My wife is in the garden, pulling small bits of vibrant, colorful life from dark soil — carrots and radishes, kale and potatoes. I watch her work, and marvel at the placidity on her face as she trims leaves and pulls fruit from vines. The garden was a whim with the new house, an experiment. I didn't know anything about gardening, but she wanted to try. She's done all the work. I've merely dug and beat back knotweed. And yet, for all our inexperience, all our not really knowing what we're doing, something amazing has begun to grow.

This love, too, is constantly beginning. I know I have a restless heart, and sometimes it wants with an unbearable ache. Sometimes I'm overwhelmed with the desire to run. And yet I stand impassive against that urge, gripping tightly to my wife, to the life we've built, terrified of what happens if it all slips away.

There is a lie in my silence, this pretense that there aren't women
for whom my blood boils, that my feelings for them are only
skin deep. But it's a lie I embrace, one I've come to hold tightly
against my chest. Love, I say, when I mean *love*, when I mean
desire's thousand paper cuts. I want, and I want, and more than
anything I want find some way to express this burning, to tell the
people who have burrowed their way into my heart how I feel,
even if I have no expectation, want nothing in return.

But while that sort of honesty is at the core of our marriage, it
can be toxic elsewhere, and I know it. One mistake, one slipped
word, and it can cause nothing but harm. And having caused
harm before, I have no wish to do so now.

I think of my acoustic guitar, gathering dust in the closet.
I think about pulling it out, finding a song that gives voice to
this muddled suffering, this ache that never seems to go away,
no matter how content I really am. I wonder if my fingers still
remember how to pluck music from the notes. I wonder, idly,
if I still have notes to play.

About the Author

Victor D. Infante is the features editor for the *Telegram & Gazette* and the editor of *Worcester Magazine* and *Worcester Living* magazine. His poems and short stories have appeared in numerous publications internationally, including *Spillway, The Chiron Review, The Collagist, Barrelhouse, Pearl* and *The Banyan Review*. His first full-length poetry collection, *City of Insomnia*, was published by Write Bloody Publications.

Acknowledgements

This book is different than anything else I've written, and it's taken a LOT of people's support and advice to get it to print, so THANK YOU to Jenna Balestrini, Derrick Brown, Tony Brown and everyone at the Outlaw Stage, Sam Cha, Kae Collins, Brendan Constantine, Oliver de la Paz, Barbara DeMarco-Barrett, Amélie Frank, Dawn Gabriel, Sarah & Dave George, Leonard Germinara, Gary Hoare, Annie Hwang, Virginia Infante, Beth Marquez, Elmo Martin, Daniel & Lori McGinn, Jenn Monroe and *Extract(s): Daily Dose of Lit*, Eric Morago, Sarah Oktay, Sara Schweiger, Kathy Silvey, Patricia Smith, Anda Volley and *Amethyst Arsenic*, Anna Woo, Bex Zumbruski, and probably a thousand other people who have helped bring this book to life. But above all, thank you my wife, Lea Deschenes, for her endless patience and support as I obsessed over this book. Thank you, thank you, thank you...

Also Available from Moon Tide Press

What Blooms in the Dark, Emily J. Mundy (2024)
Fable, Bryn Wickerd (2024)
Diamond Bars 2, David A. Romero (2024)
Safe Handling, Rebecca Evans (2024)
More Jerkumstances: New & Selected Poems, Barbara Eknoian (2024)
Dissection Day, Ally McGregor (2023)
He's a Color Until He's Not, Christian Hanz Lozada (2023)
The Language of Fractions, Nicelle Davis (2023)
Paradise Anonymous, Oriana Ivy (2023)
Now You Are a Missing Person, Susan Hayden (2023)
Maze Mouth, Brian Sonia-Wallace (2023)
Tangled by Blood, Rebecca Evans (2023)
Another Way of Loving Death, Jeremy Ra (2023)
Kissing the Wound, J.D. Isip (2023)
Feed It to the River, Terhi K. Cherry (2022)
*Beat Not Beat: An Anthology of California Poets Screwing
    on the Beat and Post-Beat Tradition* (2022)
*When There Are Nine: Poems Celebrating the Life and Achievements
    of Ruth Bader Ginsburg* (2022)
The Knife Thrower's Daughter, Terri Niccum (2022)
2 Revere Place, Aruni Wijesinghe (2022)
Here Go the Knives, Kelsey Bryan-Zwick (2022)
Trumpets in the Sky, Jerry Garcia (2022)
Threnody, Donna Hilbert (2022)
A Burning Lake of Paper Suns, Ellen Webre (2021)
Instructions for an Animal Body, Kelly Gray (2021)
Head *V* Heart: New & Selected Poems, Rob Sturma (2021)
*Sh!t Men Say to Me: A Poetry Anthology in Response
    to Toxic Masculinity* (2021)
Flower Grand First, Gustavo Hernandez (2021)
Everything is Radiant Between the Hates, Rich Ferguson (2020)
When the Pain Starts: Poetry as Sequential Art, Alan Passman (2020)
*This Place Could Be Haunted If I Didn't Believe
    in Love*, Lincoln McElwee (2020)
Impossible Thirst, Kathryn de Lancellotti (2020)
Lullabies for End Times, Jennifer Bradpiece (2020)

Crabgrass World, Robin Axworthy (2020)
Contortionist Tongue, Dania Ayah Alkhouli (2020)
The only thing that makes sense is to grow, Scott Ferry (2020)
Dead Letter Box, Terri Niccum (2019)
Tea and Subtitles: Selected Poems 1999-2019, Michael Miller (2019)
At the Table of the Unknown, Alexandra Umlas (2019)
The Book of Rabbits, Vince Trimboli (2019)
Everything I Write Is a Love Song to the World,
    David McIntire (2019)
Letters to the Leader, HanaLena Fennel (2019)
Darwin's Garden, Lee Rossi (2019)
Dark Ink: A Poetry Anthology Inspired by Horror (2018)
Drop and Dazzle, Peggy Dobreer (2018)
Junkie Wife, Alexis Rhone Fancher (2018)
The Moon, My Lover, My Mother, & the Dog,
    Daniel McGinn (2018)
Lullaby of Teeth: An Anthology of Southern California Poetry (2017)
Angels in Seven, Michael Miller (2016)
A Likely Story, Robbi Nester (2014)
Embers on the Stairs, Ruth Bavetta (2014)
The Green of Sunset, John Brantingham (2013)
The Savagery of Bone, Timothy Matthew Perez (2013)
The Silence of Doorways, Sharon Venezio (2013)
Cosmos: An Anthology of Southern California Poetry (2012)
Straws and Shadows, Irena Praitis (2012)
In the Lake of Your Bones, Peggy Dobreer (2012)
I Was Building Up to Something, Susan Davis (2011)
Hopeless Cases, Michael Kramer (2011)
One World, Gail Newman (2011)
What We Ache For, Eric Morago (2010)
Now and Then, Lee Mallory (2009)
Pop Art: An Anthology of Southern California Poetry (2009)
In the Heaven of Never Before, Carine Topal (2008)
A Wild Region, Kate Buckley (2008)
Carving in Bone: An Anthology of Orange County Poetry (2007)
Kindness from a Dark God, Ben Trigg (2007)
A Thin Strand of Lights, Ricki Mandeville (2006)
Sleepyhead Assassins, Mindy Nettifee (2006)
Tide Pools: An Anthology of Orange County Poetry (2006)
Lost American Nights: Lyrics & Poems, Michael Ubaldini (2006)

Patrons

Moon Tide Press would like to thank the following people for their support in helping publish the finest poetry from the Southern California region. To sign up as a patron, visit www.moontidepress. com or send an email to publisher@moontidepress.com.

Anonymous
Robin Axworthy
Conner Brenner
Nicole Connolly
Bill Cushing
Susan Davis
Kristen Baum DeBeasi
Peggy Dobreer
Kate Gale
Dennis Gowans
Alexis Rhone Fancher
HanaLena Fennel
Half Off Books & Brad T. Cox
Donna Hilbert
Jim & Vicky Hoggatt
Michael Kramer
Ron Koertge & Bianca Richards
Gary Jacobelly
Ray & Christi Lacoste
Jeffery Lewis
Zachary & Tammy Locklin
Lincoln McElwee
David McIntire
José Enrique Medina

Michael Miller & Rachanee Srisavasdi
Michelle & Robert Miller
Ronny & Richard Morago
Terri Niccum
Andrew November
Jeremy Ra
Luke & Mia Salazar
Jennifer Smith
Roger Sponder
Andrew Turner
Rex Wilder
Mariano Zaro
Wes Bryan Zwick

www.ingramcontent.com/pod-product-compliance
Lightning Source LLC
Chambersburg PA
CBHW031958010726
47493CB00007B/2254